GW00566755

STINGRAY

MONSTER FROM THE DEEP

STINGRAY

MONSTER FROM THE DEEP

By John Theydon

Edited by Ben Page

Anderson Entertainment Limited
The Corner House, 2 High Street, Aylesford, Kent, ME20 7BG

Stingray: Monster from the Deep by John Theydon.
First published in 1966 under the title 'Stingray and the Monster'.

Hardcover edition published by Anderson Entertainment in 2022.

www.gerryanderson.co.uk

ISBN: 9781914522239

Editorial director: Jamie Anderson
Editor: Ben Page
Cover design: Marcus Stamps

Typeset by Rajender Singh Bisht

TABLE OF CONTENTS

Chapter One

MAN FROM THE PAST

"**S**ay, Troy, that craft's there again!" growled Lieutenant Lee Sherridan, hydrophone operator of the World Aquanaut Security Patrol vessel Stingray.

Captain Troy Tempest glanced at the image of the sleek red-and-white motor launch which had appeared on the screen of the videoscan periscope above the instrument bank.

"That's the third day running," he said. "They sure must like the view, Phones."

"Yeah, looks like that girl's even taking pictures of it to put in her album."

Troy's blue eyes narrowed. "If they want picture postcards of Marineville they can get a dollar packet at any store—security checked. Let's go topside and take a closer look at them. Blow One!"

The forward tank emptied and Stingray's nose tilted. The super sub surfaced and rode gracefully on the gentle swell of the grey-green ocean in the glare of the Pacific sun.

Stingray was seaborne for a routine patrol. A mile behind, Marineville, the WASP base, was visible beyond yellow-white beaches. The checkered control tower silhouetted against the cloud-fleeced blue of the Californian sky.

Troy brought Stingray close to the launch, slowly and carefully, so that the wash did not swamp the smaller craft.

He saw the name Santa Anna and the registration number SD 21 painted on the bows. A small, swarthy-faced man in floppy panama hat, grimy white jacket and ducks was leaning against the rail. Next to him a pretty gold-tanned girl with bushy blonde hair, in a blue striped T-shirt and white shorts, was staring intently through dark sunglasses at Stingray. She held a cine-camera, with a telescopic lens.

"Registered in San Diego," Troy said. "Guess she's a bit off her beat, Phones. Okay, clear the videoscan arm. I'll go up and have a word with them."

Phones operated the control that swung the videoscan arm clear of the conning tower hatch, and Troy climbed out.

From the conning tower, he looked down on the deck of the launch. Powerful craft, he told himself. Atomic-powered turbojets. Maximum speed? Maybe two hundred knots. Easily handled by a crew of two. But somehow, this strangely contrasted pair—the pretty girl and the swarthy man in his grubby suit—did not seem to fit the picture.

"Ahoy there, Santa Anna!" he called. "What's your business?"

It was the girl who replied with a cheerful wave.

"Ahoy there, Stingray! We're just cruising around. Any law against it?"

"No, miss, but there could be against taking pictures of Marineville."

The girl pouted prettily and gestured with her camera.

"Gee, you don't think I'm a spy, planning to blow up Marineville, do you, commander?"

"I'd sure hate to think so, miss. But it's not commander," Troy grinned, tapping the three red bars on his shoulder. "Just plain captain."

"Captain?" Wonder edged the girl's voice. "Why, of course, how stupid of me! You must be Captain Tempest. The Captain Tempest! The guy who does all those wonderful things!"

"Some of the things I have to do aren't so wonderful, miss," Troy said gruffly, colouring and forcing himself to look stern. "Like ordering tourists to watch their step. Commander Shore's kind of touchy about unauthorised folk taking pictures on his front doorstep."

The girl smiled sweetly and held up the camera. "Do you want to confiscate the film, captain?"

"Guess I'll have to. Hey, wait!"

But she had already taken the roll of film from the camera. "Catch!" she called.

Her aim was almost deliberately off and the film, spilling out in a spiral as it went, fell short and dropped into the sea.

"Oh, how stupid of me!" she gasped, watching it slowly sink. "Now it's ruined!"

Then she looked up brightly at Troy. "Still, if I were a spy the pictures wouldn't be any use now, would they? Marineville can breathe again."

"Yeah!" He knew she was laughing inwardly at him, knew too, that she wasn't as dumb as she pretended to be. "You'd better pull out, miss."

She drew herself up to attention and gave him a mock salute.

"Okay, captain!" She glanced at the swarthy man beside her. "Get her underway, José."

"Si, senorita!"

José scurried away into the control cabin of the launch, and a moment later the powerful motors started up.

"Bye, Captain Tempest!" called the young woman, waving to him as the launch sped away. "Maybe we'll meet again some time."

He did not wave back but climbed down through the hatch and sat down at the controls, his tanned face set thoughtfully.

Phones winked at Marina, the lovely green-haired mysterious girl from the ocean who was the third member of Stingray's crew.

"Didn't she ask for your autograph, Troy?"

Troy grinned. "You can go to Timbuktu!"

Then he was serious again. "Something didn't add up there, Phones. She dropped that film in the water on purpose, and I've got a hunch those two weren't the only ones aboard."

"If you're suspicious, why don't we take 'em in for quizzing?"

"Reckon they're clever enough not to give us anything to pin on them. Contact control tower and have security check on their boat. Maybe we can get a line on them that way without warning 'em off. If they are up to something fishy, could be they'll hang themselves if they're given enough rope."

* * *

9

On the Santa Anna, a second man had joined the girl on deck.

He was tall and powerful, with a dark mane of grey-streaked hair sweeping back from a high intellectual brow. His heavy beard could not soften the hard, ruthless lines of his face, or completely hide the scar that ran down from his left ear lobe to the comer of his thin cruel mouth.

"Did I handle him okay, father?" the girl asked.

"Sure, Helga," he said in a harsh voice. "You handled him swell."

There was a glint in his greenish eyes as he watched the now distant Stingray submerging.

"If only we could get hold of Stingray. She's just what we need for the job. And it would hit that skunk Shore where it hurts most, losing his crack patrol vessel."

"Why not, father?" Helga said eagerly, the blue eyes behind her dark glasses now as hard as her father's.

"It's too risky to tangle with a tough guy like Tempest. We must keep our risks to the minimum, honey. It'll have to be another craft."

"Stingray or any other, I do not like this, Senor Hagen!" put in José, who had joined them.

Conrad Hagen swung on him with a contemptuous snarl.

"No one's asking you whether you like it or not, amigo. You'll do what you're told!"

"Si, si, senor!" José said hastily. "But these—how they call them?—these Wasps! They are not good to meddle with any more than those that make their nests in the jungle."

Helga smiled thinly at him. "Snap out of it, José! Just think of what's at the end of it."

José shrugged. "Si, I always think of that, senorita. At night I dream of it. It is worth taking the risks for. But, like the senor say, not with La Tempestad, as we call him down in Mexico. Caramba! José rather take on the killer shark!"

* * *

At the end of an uneventful patrol, Stingray returned to Number 3 Pen below Marineville headquarters. As Troy, Phones, and Marina came up on their seat tubes into the standby lounge a husky voice spoke over the intercom speaker,

"Control tower to Captain Tempest. Will you please report to Commander Shore immediately."

"Okay, Atlanta!" Troy replied cheerfully.

When he reached the spacious main control room, he found Commander Shore alone with his auburn-haired daughter, Atlanta, an assistant controller at WASP headquarters with the rank of lieutenant.

Shore swung his hoverchair as Troy entered and gave him a warm smile.

"Hi, Tempest! Quiet trip?"

"Yes, sir, apart from that little incident of the Santa Anna I reported."

The smile faded from Shore's craggy face. "That's what I want to see you about, captain."

He took a document his daughter handed him. "Report here from Security on that craft. It's a bona fide registration at San Diego. Owner's a guy who can be vouched for– old naval man. He says he hired it out three days ago to a Miss Helga Hansen. She said she wanted to make a sightseeing cruise up the Californian coast. She paid a deposit in cash and collected the craft with a Latin American character named José."

"That adds up, sir."

"Yeah! On the face of it an innocent little trip that plenty of folk make. Sure, you caught her taking pictures of Marineville, but I guess that's just the kind of thing a dumb tourist might do."

"She wasn't so dumb as to throw that film so that I could catch it, commander. And then, as I reported, I had a hunch somebody was keeping out of sight on that craft."

"Your hunch was right, Troy. I detailed a surface craft to keep tabs on the Santa Anna. She docked at San Renardo, forty miles south of here, about an hour later. Three people went ashore—your blonde, the man José, and this guy."

Shore signed to his daughter and she switched on the video screen. On it appeared the head-and-shoulders image of a dark-bearded man in sunglasses and panama. Even over the video screen, Troy sensed the impact of a ruthless personality.

"Know him, Tempest?"

"No, sir." Something in the commander's voice made Troy shoot a curious glance at him. "Do you, sir?"

"I've got a hunch about him. I thought of having him picked up for interrogation, but we've got nothing on him, and if he should be some innocent guy with powerful friends in Washington we'd sure get a humdinger of a rocket from the Defence Department."

"But you're still keeping tabs on him, sir?"

"That was the big idea," Shore growled. "But the numbskulls lost track. Security—bah! They couldn't keep tabs on a tortoise!"

Troy suppressed a grin. Confined to his chair since he was crippled on active service some years before, Commander Shore resented his enforced inaction while the men he commanded risked their lives in the ocean depths. At times he became irritable and short-tempered, but his men knew his bark was far worse than his bite and they worshipped him.

At a signal from him, Atlanta pressed another switch and a still shot appeared on a screen beside the first. It was of a bare-headed, hard-faced, clean-shaven man in prison clothes, with a prominent scar running down from the lobe of the left ear to the corner of his cruel mouth.

"Compare them, Tempest."

Troy studied the two faces. Strip away that beard on the one or put a beard on the other... Sure, it might be! Not easy to tell without seeing the eyes hidden by those sunglasses in the first picture.

"There's a likeness, commander. Who's the jailbird?"

"Conrad Hagen."

"Hagen?" Troy started. "That rings a bell, sir."

"It should do if you know your WASP history, Tempest. When Atlanta was a tot of three he got twenty years for piracy, without remission. He was one of the most ruthless scoundrels who ever hijacked a cargo on the seven seas— and that doesn't exclude Captain Kidd and Morgan or any of that old-time bunch of cutthroats."

"Twenty years, huh?" Troy glanced involuntarily at Shore's lovely daughter. When she was three...

He looked back at the commander. "You mean Hagen's just been released, sir?"

"Sure, a month ago. And he vanished within an hour of setting foot outside the penitentiary. Security thought he'd gone to ground someplace, but now——"

"You think he could be this bearded guy on the Santa Anna?"

"That's my hunch."

"But what's he doing up here around Marineville? This is the last place a guy like that ought to be sticking his neck out. He'd know if he put a foot wrong he'd be roped in again."

Commander Shore frowned.

"There's something maybe you don't know. A certain Captain Samuel Shore was the one who caught that tiger shark and put him behind bars. And he swore he'd get me for it if it took him the rest of his life."

"Father!" Atlanta's face had gone pale. "You never told me about this!"

"Aw, it was ancient history I guess, honey. I never lost any sleep over it. But I'm telling Troy now because maybe it could account for this guy hanging around here—if he is Hagen."

"If?" Troy repeated. "You haven't really got any doubt, have you, sir?"

Shore hesitated, then his steel-grey eyes narrowed. "No, son. You see, Hagen had a daughter when he was jailed, a blonde-haired kid about Atlanta's age. And her name was Helga."

"The girl on the Santa Anna!"

"That's my guess."

"Reckon you've got to look out for squalls, commander."

Shore slammed his fist down on the arm of his chair.

"By Neptune, I'm not scared of that guy or a hundred like him. But I don't like the notion of him being on the loose again. A tiger shark like that can't change his stripes any more than a leopard can change its spots, and we've got trouble enough with Titan breathing down our necks without having to worry about Hagen."

He drew a deep breath. "Okay, Tempest! That's all. I just figured you ought to be put wise to this guy so you can keep your eyes open for trouble. Nothing's too low for him to sink to."

Atlanta pressed a switch and the images vanished from the screens. She looked eagerly at Troy.

"I'm signing off now, Troy."

"Okay, Atlanta. I'll take you home. Maybe you and me and Phones and Marina could do a show tonight."

"That'll be swell." She took her uniform hat from her locker. "Be seeing you, father."

Commander Shore smiled fondly at her. She and the WASPs had made up his whole life since her mother had died a few years before.

"So long, honey! Have fun."

* * *

They picked up Phones and Marina and left the control building. The sun was a great ball of fire on the far rim of the Pacific Ocean.

"I'll fix a quick meal at my place," Atlanta said as they got into Troy's hovercar.

As they cruised slowly along the marine drive leading to the Shore's big house on the outskirts of Marineville, Helga Hagen, sitting at a window table in a restaurant, drew in her breath sharply.

"There goes that heel Tempest now, father," she murmured, mechanically taking the menu that the white-jacketed waiter was handing her with an obsequious bow.

At her words, the waiter's olive-skinned face tightened and a gleam of hate showed in his protruding eyes for an instant.

"Who's the redhead in WASPs' uniform in the front seat with him, I wonder?" Helga went on.

The waiter bent low and said in a winning voice, "That is Commander Shore's daughter, Atlanta, miss."

"Shore's daughter?" Conrad Hagen's bearded face lit up with an evil glint and his eyes were like chips of green ice as he watched the hovercar cruise out of sight.

The waiter took their order and sidled away. Helga looked after him curiously.

"Weird guy," she said.

"The world's full of weird birds, honey," her father said bleakly. "Especially in jail."

For some moments he sat there in silence, brooding, while Helga amused herself watching the passing traffic.

At last, he said, as if thinking aloud, "I'd give my right arm to hi-jack Stingray."

"But you said it was too risky, father."

"Sure. But I've had second thoughts. This whole thing's one mighty big gamble anyway. But if we had Stingray's speed nothing in the world could catch us underwater. The rest of the WASP vessels haven't got her fantastic speed."

He frowned. "But how to get her, that would be the problem. Security's too tight in Marineville. Somehow we'd have to try to grab her when she was at sea—"

"Excuse!"

Hagen jumped as the suave voice spoke in his ear. Neither of them had heard the soft-footed waiter return with their order.

Hagen glared at him, wondering how much he had heard. Helga was right, he was a strange bird, with his protruding eyes and strange black brows slanting down from his temples to meet in a shallow V over the bridge of his beak-like nose.

"You like to steal Stingray?" the waiter whispered, lowering his heavy lids over his gleaming eyes as he placed the food before them.

Hagen's jaw tightened and his big hands clenched beneath the table. The fool knew too much; maybe he would have to be disposed of.

But he relaxed when the whining voice went on, "I have information that will help you, sir."

After a quick glance around to see if he was observed, the waiter took from inside his white jacket a slip of paper, which he placed on the table before Hagen.

Hagen saw various navigation readings on it. "What's this?" he growled suspiciously.

"The route Stingray will take on patrol tomorrow, sir."

Hagen's eyes narrowed. "Where d'you get it?"

The waiter smiled mysteriously. "It is my business to get these things, sir."

"You fool! I could take this and not give you a cent." The waiter bowed low, rubbing his thin hands with their talon-like fingers.

"Sir, I do not want payment," he whispered. "If Tempest should die when you steal Stingray, I shall be more than repaid for my services. Heh, heh!"

Cackling to himself, the waiter moved away to the next table.

Helga looked after him suspiciously.

"He sounds like a nut-case to me, father."

"Maybe," Hagen smiled thinly as he put the slip of paper in his pocket. "But this looks like the goods to me. We won't lose anything by trying it, anyway. Let's eat up and go, honey! We've got plenty to do before morning."

* * *

When his spell of duty was over, the waiter left the restaurant, and keeping to the shadows made his way down to the beach outside Marineville. In the light of a huge moon which was coming up over the mountains, he walked along the beach to where high dark cliffs dropped sheerly down into the shimmering ocean.

A quick glance round, and he had vanished into a cleft at the base of the cliff. A few minutes later, undetected even by the radar and sound scanners that constantly protected Marineville base, a craft with a fish-like snout shot from an underwater cave and sped west.

A short time later it surfaced in a large cavern at the foot of a cliff on the lonely Isle of Lemoy. The waiter, chuckling evilly to himself, hurried ashore and entered an elevator which took him up into the old-fashioned living room of the massive century-old house which stood on the top of the cliff, and was the island's only dwelling.

Still cackling, he pressed various buttons. The elevator disappeared, a section of the floor swivelled and a gleaming instrument console and a large video screen rose smoothly into the room.

The waiter turned a control and the screen flickered and then lit up, casting a ghostly light through the room.

On the screen appeared the thin mephistophelean features of King Titan, the ruthless ruler of the underwater city of Titanica and Troy Tempest's bitter enemy.

"Well, surface agent X-20?" demanded Titan coldly, "You have something special to report that you summon me at this hour?"

The secret agent cringed low and smirked.

"Yes, O Mighty Titan! I succeeded in getting the details of the route Stingray will take on patrol tomorrow."

"Splendid!" Titan's cruel face lit up eagerly. "Give them to me, slave, and I will prepare a little surprise for the accursed Troy Tempest."

"But, Master, I have no longer got them!"

"You mean you have lost them, fool?"

"No, O Mighty One!"

The secret agent cringed so low his hideous face nearly touched the floor. "I thought of a clever scheme. There was an enemy of Tempest. He was seeking to steal Stingray, so I gave him the details of the route. He will destroy Tempest!"

"Fool! Dolt! Imbecile!" Titan raged. "It is more likely that Tempest will destroy him. If you had brought that information to me, I could have sent a squadron of mechanical fish to ambush Stingray at the most convenient point on its route. Bah! Beware, X-20! There will come a time when I shall get tired of your stupid mistakes."

And Titan vanished from the screen, leaving surface agent X-20 shivering with fear.

Chapter Two
HIGH SEAS HI-JACK

Four hundred miles west by south of Marineville an old motor yacht wallowed sluggishly in the heavy swell of the Pacific.

A few hundred yards from it a buoy, striped in grey, blue, and yellow, gleamed in the sun. The marker rolled with the waves and dipped its compact bowl antennae to all points of the compass in turn. It was one of the numerous sensitive auxiliary ears of the main tracking stations that provided a network of early warning systems for Marineville.

At the wheel of the yacht, Conrad Hagen, in a grubby sweater, slacks, and old seaman's cap, looked tight faced at his watch.

"She's scheduled to check the buoy two hours out of Marineville. She should be here soon, honey," he said to his daughter.

Dressed in jumper and jeans, her fair hair blowing in the breeze, Helga was standing at the rail, studying the water beyond the buoy through powerful binoculars.

"Sure hope you're right, father," she said. "This isn't my idea of fun. We've been all night getting here and if Stingray doesn't show up after all, it'll take us all day to get back to civilization again."

"If this boat does not sink before then," came José's scared voice from the engine room hatch. "Caramba! She leaks in every seam!"

Hagen swung on him with a snarl. "No one's asking your opinion, you lily-livered sniveller. Get back to those motors, and wait for your orders. We've got to time this just right."

José threw up his hands. "If I come out of this alive I think I go straight!"

"You rat on me now and I'll twist that bonehead of yours right off its shoulders. Get down there and stay down!"

As José disappeared below, Helga looked contemptuously after him. "I don't know why you bother to cut him in."

Hagen laughed mirthlessly. "Who's cutting him in? Right now I can't do without him. He's the only guy who can lead me to the stuff. Once we've found it…"

He left the rest unsaid, but even Helga felt a little shiver go along her spine at the merciless expression on his bearded face. She had few scruples herself. There was little she was not prepared to do at the bidding of this father whom the law had stolen from her for most of her life.

Still, at times…

She brought her mind back to the task before them, as dangerous and audacious as anything her father had attempted in his wild and lawless life.

"I didn't like that waiter guy," she said as she scanned the ocean again for the first sign of a surfacing periscope. "How do we know he can be trusted? How could he get information like that anyway? Marineville's security system is tighter than a nutshell, father."

"Any nut can be cracked," Hagen said grimly. "And Marineville's a sure-fire target for secret agents."

"Maybe, but why should this guy risk his neck getting that information and hand it on a plate to us?"

"Because he hates Tempest like I hate that skunk Shore and—"

"Here it is!"

Helga's eager cry cut like a whiplash through her father's words, and she pointed to where a faint wash was showing several hundred yards beyond the buoy.

"Action stations!" Hagen rasped, ringing down to the engine room. "Stand by that launch, honey!"

Her eyes on the surfacing submarine, Helga moved along the deck to where the yacht's only launch hung on well-oiled davits.

Her heart was pounding as she watched the glistening blue conning tower rise out of the water, then the windows of the control cabin. She grabbed her binoculars and focused them on the vessel.

"Father! she cried. "It's not—"

A dull boom from below smothered her voice, and José, his face a ghastly grey, shot out of the engine room hatch, dark smoke pouring after him.

He rushed for the boat and grabbed frantically at the davit ropes.

"Quick! We will sink!"

Helga's hand flashed to the pocket of her jeans and a small gun seemed to blossom from it.

"Stand back, José," she said in a brittle voice. "You lower the boat in a panic and it'll capsize." She smiled tightly. "Women and children first."

Hagen, joining them, sneered at the shivering man.

"That's swell, José! You being in a blue funk will help to pull the wool over Tempest's eyes."

Helga remembered what she was going to tell him when the explosion occurred.

"Tempest won't be on that sub, father. It's not Stingray!"

"What?"

Hagen swung to look at the WASP vessel, which had now fully surfaced and was cruising towards them. His face twisted in a snarl of baffled rage when he saw the number 13 marked clearly on the upper fins at the rear of the cabin.

"That fool of a waiter!"

The yacht gave a violent lurch and a gout of steam erupted from the engine room hatch.

"Into the boat," he snapped. "We've got no choice now."

Quickly, the lifeboat was launched. Even as the motor propelled it away from the side, the yacht heeled over and the wash hurled the launch towards the approaching submarine. It capsized, flinging the three occupants into the water.

José screamed in terror. He surfaced, arms flailing, and splashed his way to the upturned boat, where Hagen and Helga were already clinging.

Hagen looked at him contemptuously. "For a guy who cracks he's been down as far as you have, you're mighty scared of the water, José."

"Diving in the swim gear is one thing. This is another," spluttered the South American. "I cannot breathe air and water at the same time."

"Sometimes I reckon it's a pity you have to breathe at all," Hagen snarled.

With a vicious hissing of steam and a muffled explosion, the yacht slid down beneath the waves.

"Ahoy there! Hold on and we'll fish you out."

The skipper of WASP Vessel 13 was calling down to them from the conning tower. As the submarine edged closer a rope came snaking down.

Helga grabbed it and was hauled up.

Captain Mikayla Stuart looked at her admiringly. Even wet and bedraggled, Helga was still beautiful.

"You okay, miss?"

Helga smiled weakly, "I—I guess so, captain. Oh, it was terrible! If—if you hadn't happened to be around, I don't know what would have happened. The sharks…"

She patted her shoulder. "Take it easy! You're okay now. Get below and my hydrophone operator will fix you up with hot coffee, while I fish your menfolk out."

A few moments later Hagen and José were in the conning tower.

Stuart looked curiously at Hagen.

"Say, haven't I seen you someplace before, mister?"

Hagen smiled thinly. "I don't remember having had the pleasure, captain," he said, sliding his hand casually into the watertight pocket of his slacks.

Suddenly Mikayla's face hardened. "I've got it! You're the guy whose picture Security issued yesterday. They warned us to look out for you."

"I'm flattered," Hagen said harshly. And drawing his gun, he shot the WASP captain.

"Over the side with her," he ordered as Stuart collapsed with a groan.

José, his face pale, lifted the wounded woman and heaved her out of the conning tower into the water.

In the cabin, the hydrophone operator, Lieutenant Rod Anderson, heard the shot and swung round.

"What the…"

"Take it easy, lieutenant," said Helga.

He glanced at her, his eyes widening in amazement when he saw the small gun levelled at him.

"It may look like a toy," she said, "but it makes a man-sized hole. Get topside! I reckon your buddy needs company."

His teeth set, Anderson climbed up into the conning tower. Powerful arms gripped him and he was heaved, struggling, into the water, where Mikayla Stuart, swimming feebly in the red-tinged water, was drifting slowly astern.

"The sharks will soon scent your comrade's blood," Hagen called down to Anderson. He laughed mirthlessly. "You should have quite an interesting time."

Lieutenant Anderson turned and swam towards Stuart, reaching her just as she was about to go down again. He trod water and shouted up at the sneering bearded figure in the conning tower.

"You won't get away with this, you skunk. The Wasps will get you, wherever you are,"

A mocking laugh floated over the water, and then Hagen disappeared into the hatch. A few moments later, Patrol Vessel 13 slid smoothly beneath the waves.

Anderson looked about him despairingly. The capsized launch was low in the water and even as he calculated his chances of reaching it, the craft sank out of sight.

"Leave me, Rod!" Mikayla gasped, "I—I'm done for, anyway."

"Not on your Nellie!" Anderson growled. His eyes lit up as he caught sight of the bobbing tracker buoy several hundred yards away. "Come on, pal! We're gonna make it! We'll beat that murdering shark yet!"

* * *

In Wasp 13, Conrad Hagen sat in the captain's seat, smiling with malicious satisfaction as he methodically checked the controls and listed equipment.

"...sting missiles...two aquasprites...two monocopters...swim gear. She's got the lot, Helga! Too bad she isn't Stingray, but we'll take some catching all the same." He consulted the navigation charts. "Course 103 north-north-east."

"Northeast? I thought we were heading south, father!"

He smiled coldly. "Not yet, honey. First, we return to Marineville."

"Marineville? Have you gone crazy? As soon as this craft's reported missing—"

"The last place they'll search will be the waters around Marineville, Helga. But that's not my real reason for returning. As we have not got the fastest underwater craft in the world, we'll need a safeguard in case we're pursued."

"What kind of a safeguard?"

"A hostage."

"El diablo!" exclaimed José, wringing his thin hands agitatedly. "Now we put our heads into the mouth of the lion!"

"Shut up, you!" Hagen snarled at him, "Get below and rustle up something to eat."

"Si, senor!"

Muttering to himself, José scampered down the companionway to the galley on the lower deck.

Helga frowned after him. "I'm beginning to think our jittery amigo is going to be something of a liability."

"All the more reason why we should have a hostage."

"Why not one of those two WASPs?"

Hagen shook his head. "No good. It needs to be somebody whose precarious position will influence my old amigo Commander Shore. And I have the perfect subject in mind."

Hagen laughed evilly, and he triggered maximum speed.

* * *

Atlanta was due to report for duty at ten o'clock. She did a few necessary chores and left the house with ample time to walk the few miles along the Marine drive to headquarters.

As she stepped briskly out, a trim figure in her grey WASP uniform, a sleek hovercar drew up with a whisper of sound beside her and a blonde girl behind the controls put her head from the window.

"Could I give you a lift, lieutenant?"

Atlanta regarded her curiously. The girl was a stranger to her and there was something about her pretty face that she didn't like.

"No, thank you!" she smiled. "I'm enjoying the walk."

"You'll ride!" rasped a voice from the rear of the car. "But I won't promise you'll enjoy it."

A cold hand seemed to close about Atlanta's heart when she saw the gun pointing at her over the edge of the lowered window. Behind it a ruthless bearded face stared up at her– a face she remembered having seen before.

"Conrad Hagen!" she gasped and looked about her desperately. The road was deserted except for another car speeding away from them.

"Get in, lieutenant!" Hagen ordered harshly. "I shall have no compunction about killing the daughter of Commander Shore, although I prefer to have her company on a little trip I'm about to make."

Atlanta knew he wasn't making an idle threat. Her mouth dry, she got into the rear of the car when Hagen pushed the door open. He slammed it after her and pulled down the blinds.

"Okay, Helga!" he said. "Let's go."

* * *

Troy Tempest roamed the luxurious stand-by lounge at WASP headquarters like a caged animal.

Phones looked up from the book he was reading and exchanged smiles with Marina, who was doing an electronic puzzlegram.

"Relax, pal!" he said.

"Relax, nothing!" Troy retorted. "Off duty's the time for relaxing. Standing by indefinitely, just because the old man's got a hunch that guy Hagen might make trouble— Aw, it's getting me down! Patrol duty's better than this. At least there's a chance of running up against a Titan terror fish."

"Control tower to Stingray crew!" cut in a voice from the intercom speaker. "Report to Commander Shore at once, please."

Troy grabbed his cap and hurried out.

"Now he's happy!" Phones chuckled to Marina, as they followed.

When Troy entered the control room, Shore and Lieutenant Fisher were studying the big wall chart of the Pacific. Troy was surprised to see that Atlanta wasn't there. A vague uneasiness stirred in his mind.

"Where's Atlanta, sir?" he asked. Shore swung his chair towards him.

"Confound Atlanta!" the commander barked. "She's late for duty. Spent too long fixing her hair, I guess. She'll get a rocket when she does show up, my daughter or not… Tempest, Number Thirteen's missing!"

Immediately, Troy forgot Atlanta. "Thirteen? That's Mikayla Stuart's craft, the one that took over Stingray's patrol chore this morning!"

"Yeah. Stuart should have checked in a routine report half an hour ago. We've heard nothing. We've tried to contact them, but there's no reply."

"You suspect Conrad Hagen, sir?"

Shore frowned. "I wouldn't have thought Hagen had a craft powerful enough to attack a WASP vessel, captain. Not to sink it without a trace, but—launch Stingray and proceed to investigate. The lieutenant will give you the last known location of Thirteen."

"Okay, sir."

"Hold it!" exclaimed Fisher. "Message coming through."

A voice came over the radio speaker. "Lieutenant Anderson to control tower. Lieutenant Anderson to control tower…"

The signal was faint as if the transmitter lacked power.

Shore grabbed his microphone. "Come in, lieutenant. Where the blazes are you speaking from?"

"Tracker buoy twenty-seven, sir!"

"What? You should have cleared that nearly two hours ago."

"I'm on the buoy itself, sir, transmitting from it. It's taken me all this time to tap the tracker circuit. Captain Stuart's in a bad way. Shot. That guy Conrad Hagen tricked us, hi-jacked the sub—"

The rest of Anderson's words were lost in an explosion of energy from Shore.

"Sound action stations!" he roared to his assistant. "All combat craft to stand by. Send a plane to pick up those two officers and alert every submarine and surface craft within a thousand-mile radius of tracker buoy twenty-seven. Number Thirteen must be located and Hagen arrested."

"Yes, sir!"

Fisher leapt to the massive control console and Troy looked eagerly at Commander Shore.

"Any special orders for Stingray, sir?"

"Yeah! Stand by with the rest."

"But, sir—"

"I said standby, Tempest! When Number Thirteen's located you'll get your orders, not before."

"Sir!" Fisher looked around eagerly from the console, where a red light was flashing. "Something's coming through on Number Thirteen's videoscan wavelength."

"What?" Shore thundered. "Switch on the screen!"

As the lieutenant obeyed, the big video screen sprang to life and on it materialised the ruthless bearded face of Conrad Hagen.

"So, we meet again, Shore, if you can call it a meeting," he said harshly. "I had hoped to come to closer grips with you then this after twenty long years of nursing my hate. But I can wait a little longer for the pleasure— Hold it, Shore!"

His rasping voice rang through the control room as Shore raised his hand to signal to his assistant.

"Don't try to trace my position, Shore. And call off that all-vessels alert!"

Shore scowled, jaw jutting pugnaciously. "I don't take orders from guys like you, Hagen. I'll put you back behind bars."

"I don't think so." Hagen jeered. "Just take a look at what I have here in the cabin of Number Thirteen."

His image vanished from the screen and was replaced by that of Atlanta, her lovely face pale, powerful hands gripping her arms.

"Call off the search for me, Shore!" snarled Hagen's voice, "or I'll feed her to the sharks."

Chapter Three
GO GET HAGEN!

Troy felt his heart contract as he looked at Atlanta's image on the screen.

Commander Shore's rugged face suffused with rage.

"By thunder, Hagen, if you don't bring her ashore and give yourself up—"

"Don't talk like a fool, Shore!" Hagen's voice was contemptuous now. "You're in no position to make threats. I hold all the cards. I'm giving you five minutes to make up your mind. If I don't hear that cancellation signal go out—"

"Don't take any notice of him, father!" Atlanta cried. "He's bluffing. He wouldn't dare—"

She broke off, her hazel eyes widening in terror, as a swarthy hand holding a long thin knife appeared before her on the screen and the point was placed against her throat.

"I'm not bluffing, Shore!" Hagen snarled. "And you know it. I'll be listening for that cancellation. And don't try sending any code messages. If I find your hounds on my trail, your daughter dies."

The screen went blank, but the image of Atlanta's terrified face was still in front of Troy's mind, and a cold hatred of Hagen welled up in him.

"What are you aiming to do, sir?" Troy demanded hoarsely.

Shore's face had drained of colour. Suddenly he seemed to have aged ten years. He looked at Troy like a man in a dream.

"Do?" he repeated heavily, passing a hand over his face as if trying to clear his mind. "If I do my duty, Tempest, I'll order all craft to go ahead and hunt down that worthless eel and destroy him!"

Troy's throat went tight. He knew the commander put duty before all else.

"But—but Atlanta, sir!" he gasped. "You just can't condemn your own daughter to death!"

"No, I can't!" Shore growled. "I'd sooner ask to be relieved of my command. But Hagen can't be allowed to get away with this, Tempest."

He signalled to Fisher. "Call off the alert, lieutenant!"

"Yes, sir!"

As the message went out, Shore looked grimly at Troy. "There's just one exception to that order—Stingray! She's our only hope, Tempest. We've got to take a gamble on her. Go get Hagen—and get him good!"

Troy drew himself up and saluted, shocked by the mingled grief and hatred he saw in his commander's steel grey eyes.

"Okay, sir! I'll get him—and bring Atlanta back!"

Fisher stopped Troy as he was about to leave the control room with Phones and Marina and handed him a slip from his memo pad.

"Hagen couldn't have known that all calls to Marineville are tracked and logged automatically," he said. "Here's the position that video call came from, captain."

Troy glanced at it. "South-south-west 107, reference 16. Guess that's roughly a hundred miles from Marineville, lieutenant?"

"Sure, but the video source was moving southwest fast."

"Not as fast as Stingray can move," Troy said grimly. "The auto-locator on Thirteen's not working, I reckon?"

"Can't be, or we'd have traced her earlier. Hagen must have found it and disconnected it. So you'll be fishing blind, captain."

"Yeah! But we'll find him, lieutenant. If it takes a million years!"

* * *

"Million years could be right," Phones said as they hurried into the stand-by lounge. "It'll be like looking for a particular bit of driftwood in the Sargasso Sea, Troy. That shark, Hagen, could be heading to any point of the compass right now."

"I'm playing a hunch he'll change course to the southeast." Troy strapped himself in his injector seat. "Don't forget he's got a South American guide with him. Guess that was his hand holding the knife at Atlanta's throat. So I'm thinking there's a tie-up down there somewhere."

"You could be right. And I can't see Hagen hijacking a WASP vessel unless he wanted it mighty bad for something. You reckon he's going pirate again?"

"Maybe. But my guess is he needs it to get somewhere deep. Otherwise he could have used that launch he hired."

"That sure adds up, Troy."

Drum beats sounded over the intercom, and Troy glanced round to make sure that Marina was in her seat. The girl from the sea flashed him an eager smile. She was as anxious as he and Phones to go to the rescue of her friend Atlanta.

"Launch stations!" Troy said, pressing a button on his seat.

The hydraulic tubes lowered them swiftly into Stingray's control cabin. When the hatches were closed and the hydroplanes set, Troy spoke to the control tower.

"Ready to launch!"

"Clear to go!" replied Fisher.

"Release elevators!" Troy ordered. Stingray began to slide down into the deep water of its pen. "Rate one, Phones!"

The atomic generator started up and Stingray glided into the narrow launch tunnel leading to the ocean door.

"Clear to leave Marineville!"

The massive round door opened to allow the super sub to hurtle into the dark depths of the Pacific.

"Seaborne!" Troy said.

It was Commander Shore who replied this time, his voice gruff with anxiety.

"Listen, Tempest! You're on your own from now on. If we maintain radio or video contact, Hagen will know you're on his tail, and Atlanta—"

He said no more, but Troy knew what he meant. "Okay, sir! We're on our way. When you do hear from us, it'll be to report mission accomplished."

"Good luck, Troy!"

And with that laconic remark, all communication between Stingray and the outside world was severed.

Troy took the mighty vessel beyond territorial waters and then swung her south-by-west.

"Rate six, Phones!"

At maximum underwater speed of six hundred knots, Stingray flashed through the deep blue of the ocean's twilight zone. About ten minutes later, Phones spoke up.

"Guess this is it, Troy. Position 107, reference sixteen."

"Okay! Cut to reconnaissance cruise, Phones. From now on we're looking for that proverbial needle in the haystack—without a magnet."

* * *

On the Isle of Lemoy, Surface agent X-20 switched on his video screen. After a moment, the aquiline features of King Titan appeared on it.

"Well, slave? What news have you for me this time?"

"O Mighty Titan!" whined X-20, "I have just learned through my secret channels that the bearded stranger did not seize Stingray. Something must have gone wrong."

"Imbecile!" sneered Titan. "Doesn't it occur to your prawn brain that perhaps your information was false? Bah! It was well that you didn't give it to me, after all."

"Yes, master. But the bearded stranger seized another WASP vessel—and he has the daughter of Commander Shore on board as a hostage."

"Splendid! This Terrainean sounds a creature after my own heart. He would make a good ally. Why has he stolen the vessel?"

"I do not know, O Mighty One. But he is heading southwest, and Commander Shore has sent Troy Tempest after him."

"Tempest!" Titan's face was distorted by a spasm of hatred. "I would give half my kingdom to get Tempest in my power. To see him grovelling here at my feet begging for mercy, to see him suffering the torture of the lobster rack and the fire coral and the swordfish chamber, before letting him die the lingering death of a thousand stings. Tell me, slave! Is Stingray alone on this mission?"

"Yes, your Majesty! The bearded stranger has threatened to kill Shore's daughter if a search is made for him. So Stingray has been secretly launched and is no longer in contact with Marineville."

"Ah!" Titan's eyes gleamed maliciously. "So if Stingray is in trouble, no one will come to its aid. You have done well, X-20. Perhaps, after all, you are a little less stupid than you look."

The surface agent bowed low. "Thank you, O Mighty Titan! You are generous."

* * *

Switching off the video, Titan gathered his green robe about him and sat down on his pearl-studded throne. He picked up a coral gavel and struck a massive conch shell hanging beside him. As the sound echoed away through the empty chamber, an aquaphibian appeared, bowing low before him.

It was one of the many hideous primitive underwater creatures– part man, part crustacean– that served Titan and provided the crews for the terror fish with which he waged constant war against the surface people whom he hated and desired to conquer and enslave.

"Yes, O Mighty Titan?" the creature said in a gurgling, sing-song voice. "You have orders for me?"

"Alert all mechanical fish crews south of Marineville to be on the lookout for Stingray."

The creature's protruding fish eyes glinted savagely.

"You wish it destroyed, O Mighty One?"

"If there is no choice. But if Tempest and his crew— particularly that wretch, Marina, who was once my slave— are brought here alive, there shall be great rewards."

"I shall relay your Majesty's orders!" the aquaphibian said, bowing himself out of the throne room with a faint rasping of his green hide.

* * *

Atlanta had no idea how long she had been a prisoner. Three, maybe four hours? Bound hand and foot, she lay on a bunk in the crew's sleeping quarters on the lower deck of WASP Thirteen, listening close to the whine of the atomic generator driving the twin hydro jets.

Although her duties mainly confined her to base, she was no stranger to operational craft and could judge their speed fairly accurately from the pitch of the motors.

"Around four hundred knots," she mused. "Near maximum for this craft. She's going to take some catching. Only Stingray could do it."

Her heart leapt at the thought of the WASP's crack patrol vessel and the man who captained it. In spite of Hagen's threat, she knew her father would not hold his hand completely. She had worked with him long enough to know how his mind would operate in a crisis like this. He'd call off the general alert but would give Troy a free hand as he had so often done before.

But even Troy, with the super-power of Stingray at his command, was going to have his work cut out for him. Locating a fast-moving underwater craft in the millions of cubic miles of ocean that stretched away south and west of Marineville, clear down to Antarctica might be beyond any aquanaut's abilities.

If there were some way to give him a lead! In old time movies the heroine would contrive to drop a trail of paper or peas or something equally convenient left handy for her by the stupid villains.

But how could she, bound on a bunk in the depths of the ocean, leave a trail? And, villain though Conrad Hagen was, stupid he certainly wasn't.

She looked round as the door of the cabin opened. Helga Hagen stood there, regarding her with a cynical smile.

" 'Don't take any notice of him, father! He's bluffing,' " she mimicked. "You little fool! If you knew my father as well as your wretched father does, you'd realise he never bluffs."

Atlanta said nothing. She got no consolation from the thought that she was not the only girl aboard. She sensed that, although they had never met before, Helga hated her just because she was Commander Shore's daughter. This was a blind, unreasoning hatred inspired by a warped sense of loyalty to her own evil father.

Helga moved towards the bunk, drawing a knife from a sheath at her slim waist. There was such a ferocious expression on her face that involuntarily Atlanta shrank back.

The other girl burst into shrill laughter.

"Fool! You think my father would want you killed? You are too useful to him. He wants to talk to you. Come!"

She slashed the cords binding Atlanta's ankles and helped her roughly to her feet, then pushed her to the door.

As she stumbled awkwardly up the companionway to the control cabin with her hands still tied behind her back, Atlanta feverishly calculated her chances of turning the tables on her captors. But what hope had she against the three of them? Helga might be right about her being too useful to Hagen for him to want her killed, but she had no doubt he would be ruthless with her if she gave him cause.

José was sitting in the stand-by lounge cleaning his dirty fingernails with the point of a long knife. His dark crafty eyes touched her for an instant and then slid away as if he were afraid to meet her gaze.

José was a scoundrel, she told herself, and she was sure he had no guts. He was the weak link here. She wondered if she could make use of that fact.

Hagen was at the controls. He looked round as she approached and indicated the vacant hydrophone operator's seat beside him.

"Sit down!" he said harshly.

She obeyed. A faint crackling came from the radio speaker. A persistent pinging, alternately fading and swelling, came from the sound scanners as they located rock outcrops and other obstacles. In the light of the vessel's searchlight beams, grotesque fish suddenly appeared and were swept away into the slipstream. The depth gauge showed they were three hundred fathoms down.

Instinctively, her glance went to the two-way radio switch. If the transmitter was alive, a shouted S.O.S. might be picked up by Marineville or by another vessel or a tracking station that would locate the stolen vessel.

Hagen must have read her thoughts. "You don't think I'd be stupid enough to give you the chance to send a message?" he jeered. He opened a flap on the control bank and showed her the end of a disconnected coaxial cable. "The transmitter's not working. I don't need it. I never take unnecessary risks, Miss Shore."

She said nothing. One cry for help wouldn't be much use anyway. At the speed it was travelling the submarine would be far away by the time vessels could be rushed to the point. And what if Hagen carried out his threat to throw her to the sharks?

Hagen went on, "You are a lieutenant in the WASPs. You will act as a navigator for me. I'm not familiar with these waters."

She looked at him defiantly. "Aren't you afraid I'd trick you?"

"No, Miss Shore, for two reasons. If you sabotaged the vessel you would die with us. And if we didn't die I should see that you did—unpleasantly. Very, very unpleasantly."

He spoke casually, a smile touching his lips, but there was something about his voice and in his greenish eyes that sent an icy prickling down her spine.

She hesitated, her instinct being to refuse to help him.

And then she remembered something that set her pulse racing and made her lower her eyes for fear he should see the gleam of hope in them.

"Okay," she said with feigned resignation. "But I'll need my hands free."

He signed to Helga, who was standing behind her, and the other girl cut the cords about her wrists.

"Don't try to be clever," Hagen warned her as he watched her rubbing her wrists to restore the circulation, "Doublecross me and Helga will shoot you, won't you, honey?"

Helga uttered a hard little laugh and drew her gun. "Right in the back of that red head," she said maliciously.

Atlanta shuddered. The girl might be putting on an act, but how could she be sure of that?

"Where are we heading?" she asked, forcing herself to speak casually.

"There's no need for you to know our exact destination, lieutenant!" Hagen put sardonic emphasis on the word. "For the present it is sufficient that we head south-southeast, at near maximum speed and in fairly deep water."

South-south-east? Atlanta realised that meant tacking almost at ninety degrees to their present course. If her plan was to work effectively she must make her first move at the point where they changed heading.

She calculated their present position, approximately seven hundred miles west of Mexico and twelve hundred miles south-by-west of Marineville. She took her time charting a course for

Hagen, keying herself up for what she planned to do. She must not arouse the slightest suspicion.

"Okay," she said at length. "Steer 267 east, 378 south." As he concentrated on changing course, Atlanta held her breath and felt with her toe for a press button at the base of the instrument bank. It was isolated from the main controls for emergency use if the instruments were out of action and the vessel was unable to surface.

She depressed the button and withdrew her toe. Only then did she breathe again. Neither Hagen, concentrating on his controls, nor his daughter, warily watching Atlanta's hands, had been aware of the surreptitious move.

"Caramba!" José exclaimed from the standby lounge.

"What's eating you?" Hagen snarled, glaring round at the man, who was peering upwards from the window behind the couch on which he was sitting.

"Senor! Such a strange fish, like I never see before. He go up like a bomb—whoosh!"

"Numb, skull! If you're going to let off steam like that every time you see a strange fish—"

"Si, senor, but—"

"Shut up!"

As José subsided into silence, Atlanta thanked her stars it had been José who had seen the radio beacon buoy she had released from its bay, and not Hagen, who might have recognised it for what it was.

* * *

Troy glanced at the image of the buoy gradually becoming clearer on the periscope video screen.

"It's Number Thirteen, all right, Phones," he said.

"Sure hope it doesn't mean what it usually does, Troy."

Troy grunted agreement. Only in the direst emergencies were the S.O.S. buoys released to transmit their urgent messages. The craft they were hunting might now be a crushed and twisted wreck many thousands of feet deep and Atlanta—

"Guess we'd better take a look below."

"Hold it, Troy!" Phones broke in eagerly. "There's another S.O.S. coming through from Number Thirteen. Signal strength indicates range nine hundred to one thousand miles."

Troy felt relief surge through him. "So it's still in one piece and travelling mighty fast. It's just over two hours since we first tracked this buoy. What's the location of the second?"

Phones studied his tracking instruments, "It's about the middle of Albatross Plateau."

"That's almost due south-south-east from here." Troy said, looking at a chart of the central Pacific. "Seems he's heading across the equator, making for South America, just as I figured he would."

"But I don't get it, Troy. Why's he letting those buoys go?"

Troy frowned, "It sure doesn't seem to make sense. Hagen can't be that crazy. The first one might have been released by accident, but—"

He looked round as Marina gripped his shoulder. She had been listening to their conversation, unable to join in because she was dumb, but now she gestured eagerly to Troy.

"Atlanta?" he exclaimed. "You reckon it's Atlanta who's released those buoys, Marina? Sure, it's the only explanation that makes sense. Somehow she's got to the controls and she's blazing a trail for us."

He turned back to Phones. "Set course for that buoy. We can home in on its signals. Rate five."

* * *

Back in Marineville, Fisher turned from the instrument console to look at Commander Shore, puzzled.

"Another S.O.S. from Number Thirteen, sir, nine hundred and eighty three miles south-south-east of the first."

"Yeah?" For the first time since he had seen his daughter's terrified face on the video screen before him, Shore brightened. "That's my girl!"

"You mean—"

"Sure. Atlanta's behind this, lieutenant. Who else? That shark Hagen would be covering his trail, not broadcasting it."

"What are you going to do, sir?"

"Nothing, just nothing, lieutenant." Shore smiled grimly. "Stingray will be on the job already, I guess, and heaven help Hagen when Tempest catches up with him."

Chapter Four
INTO THE ABYSS

Nearly two hours later, Phones reported, "Maximum signal strength now, Troy. Guess that second buoy's almost overhead. Where do we go from here?"

Troy considered. There should be two buoys left in the bays of the fleeing submarine. Atlanta wouldn't waste them. The first one had marked a change of course. The odds were this one did too. From here, far out in the Pacific, their quarry could have gone in any direction.

"Guess Hagen wouldn't have doubled back on his tracks," he told Phones. "And I can't see him heading west. I'm still playing my hunch that he's making for South America."

"Boy, that's a whale of a coastline! What do we do, shut our eyes and stick a pin in the chart?"

"We could hang around waiting to see if Atlanta sends out another marker buoy, but we'll take a chance, Phones. It's my bet Hagen would veer east rather than south. Steer a course for the Galapagos Islands. We can change course again if we get another signal. Rate three!"

* * *

They were a hundred miles from the Galapagos when they picked up the third buoy's signals.

"You weren't far off target," Phones said. "This one's approximately eight hundred miles south-south-east, near the start of the Peru-Chile Trench, I guess."

Troy traced the line of the great underwater canyon with his finger on the chart before him.

"That could make sense, Phones. Seems to bear out my theory that Hagen hi-jacked that sub so he could go deep."

"Well, he's sure got plenty to play around with there, pal. Three thousand miles of it, four miles deep in places."

"Yeah. But if he's down there, we'll find him. Rate six, Phones. He's still two hours ahead of us. We've got to try to make up some of that time now."

The sound of Stingray's motors deepened from a steady hum to a quivering roar, then rose rapidly to a screaming whine as the super sub hurtled through the depths of the Pacific.

* * *

Just over an hour later they neared the vast submarine trench which runs parallel to the shoreline of South America, plunging as deep into the ocean bed as the peaks of the mighty Andes rear above the surface, and forming with them one colossal slope eight miles high in places and three thousand miles long.

Phones said presently, "That buoy's right ahead, Troy, five miles maybe. Allowing for the northward current drift, I guess she started way back in the trench."

"Cut to cruise rate one, Phones. How much water is below us?"

"Six thousand feet, shelving rapidly to ten."

"Okay, we'll play it deep from now on. Stand by!"

Smoothly, the super sub glided down at a steep angle like a giant fish towards the ocean bed far below. Troy switched off all but the instrument bank lights. The enemy they believed to be somewhere in the great trench ahead of them had scanners as efficient as those aboard Stingray. He couldn't give him the additional advantage of a well-lit target at which to aim his torpedoes.

Marina came forward and stood at his shoulder, peering ahead into the darkening water. Born in the depths of the ocean, she could see and hear things that surface humans could not, and to the Stingray crew, she was better than an extra scanning device.

"Five hundred feet!" reported Phones, watching his depth gauge. "Six hundred. . . ."

Even at cruise rate, they were descending swiftly. Already the deep blue of the twilight zone was beginning to fade as they entered the depths below the continental shelf line.

A porbeagle shark loomed up with huge mouth agape, as if curious about this strange monster that was invading its hunting grounds, and then with a flick of its great tail was gone.

Eight hundred... nine... one thousand...

A giant squid, a mere baby, fifteen feet long, flashed past like a half-glimpsed vision from a nightmare world.

Eleven hundred... twelve... thirteen...

The sea was a dead grey, fading gradually into inky blackness. There were few shoal fish to be seen. The darkness was relieved only by drifting specks of zooplankton and decayed organic matter that reflected the faint light from the cabin like tiny flakes of snow.

Eighteen hundred feet...

There was no sound but the whine of the generator and the pinging of the sound-scanner registering the depth.

A starry flash of phosphorescence showed off to port at the limit of their light halo. Then a bluish-green flare drifted past, looking, Troy thought, like a tiny sun in the black void of space.

He smiled. Men like Steve Zodiac could keep their outer space when he had a world like this to explore. Odd, he thought, how even in the twenty-first century humanity knew more about the other planets of the solar system than he did of the vast depths of the ocean which covered seven-tenths of their own planet.

"Two thousand!" intoned Phones. "Getting a mighty lot of plankton whisper, Troy. It's going to screen the scanners."

"It'll be the same for Hagen."

They were completely out of the twilight zone now, descending into the zone of eternal night in which no plant life existed and whose few grotesque creatures were seldom big enough to be the menace they looked.

But Troy knew they could take nothing on chance. Occasionally, Nature hatched out some horrific mutations in the abyssal zone. There had been times when even Stingray had come near to disaster in an encounter with one of these nightmares of the deep.

"Three thousand!" announced Phones.

Suddenly the monotonous 'ping-ping' of the sound scanner registering the depth took on a deeper, agitated note. A grey smudge appeared on the chart.

"Rock sounding," Phones said. "Nine hundred feet ahead. Looks like we're heading for a cliff."

"Must be the entrance to the trench," Troy said, his pulses quickening slightly.

Once they entered that great gash in the sea bed danger would stalk them at every foot of the way.

No sound scanner could detect an enemy craft lurking behind a rock outcrop, for the rock would throw back the echo screening whatever lay behind it. The first warning they'd get would be the rapid pinging of a torpedo flashing at them, and Troy would have to rely on his own quick reactions to avoid disaster.

The other cliff was registering on the scanner now. The gap was scarcely half a mile wide and Troy knew it could not be the main trench, but a subsidiary canyon. The ocean bed shelved steeply towards it.

Stingray entered it at ten thousand feet and levelled off a few hundred feet above the bottom, nosing slowly into the unknown, keeping close to the starboard wall. It rose sheer above them, bare and smooth, slashed here and there by crevices from which occasionally flashed a tiny fish with rows of lights gleaming like portholes in a miniature submarine liner.

Twenty miles into the canyon, Phones said eagerly, "Picking up another buoy signal, Troy."

"Number Four. That's the last, the important one maybe, Phones. How far ahead?"

"Seven or eight hundred miles, I guess. Not easy to tell—— these rock walls cause too much wave deflection."

It was many years since Marineville scientists had been able to overcome the distortion that water caused to radio waves, so that submarine communications over great distances were possible, but rock formations were still an obstacle to accurate underwater tracking.

Troy whistled softly. "They've gained on us some, Phones. We've been playing it too careful."

He consulted the chart of the southeast Pacific. "Guess that puts it around the Peru-Chile border. We can afford to get a move on. Rate——"

Marina's hand closed tightly on his shoulder. She was leaning forward, pointing down the canyon, looking at something beyond the limited range of the faint light.

"Searchlight, Phones!" he snapped.

The powerful beams stabbed out, lighting up the canyon hundreds of feet ahead.

And then Troy saw what Marina must have already seen. Rising from the ooze just ahead of them was a huge drag-net.

Had they accelerated to rate four, as he'd been about to order, Stingray would have gone slap into it.

"Stand by! Emergency stations!"

He sent Stingray screaming up in a steep climb, and its skids tore through the top of the net.

"Mechanical fish!" Phones yelled.

Troy caught a glimpse of a sinister, spiky fish-shape with big glaring eyes, hurtling from behind the huge rock where it had been lurking.

"Stand by! Sting missiles!" he ordered, sending Stingray into an almost vertical climb at four hundred knots.

In the videoscan screen, he saw Titan's terror fish climbing rapidly on his tail, seeking to get it in line with the gaping mouth through which its deadly torpedo weapons were fired.

He flung Stingray backwards in a loop. Hurtling upside down over the terror fish, he saw a torpedo flash from its mouth and vanish into the darkness of the water above.

As he brought Stingray swooping round, a dull boom came over the hydrophones. Shock waves registered on the graphs. Somewhere above, the missile had hit the cliff face.

Then Troy was climbing after the enemy craft, closing in rapidly on its tail. It twisted and turned as the terrified aquaphibian at the controls tried to evade that relentless pursuit, but always the greater speed of the WASP vessel frustrated its efforts.

"Fire port sting missile," Troy said bleakly.

The slim missile hurtled from its tube, homing on its target. The enemy pilot made one last desperate attempt to avoid it, but even as the terror fish swung to the left, the sting missile struck it amidships and the dark water was rent by a vivid red and yellow flash.

Troy dived steeply to avoid the glowing debris and the scanners pinged another warning.

"Terror fish two degrees to starboard, ten fathoms down, climbing fast," Phones reported flatly.

"Stand by to fire starboard missile!" Troy ordered, changing course slightly to the right.

The terror fish came into the light beams, hurtling towards them. Through its port eye, Troy saw the hideous green face of the pilot, contorted with hate and rage.

Troy knew the advantage was his, for the Titan craft was too low to get Stingray in its sights.

"Fire!" he ordered.

Again a sting missile sped true to its target, right into the gaping mouth. The terror fish disintegrated in a vivid yellow-red flare as its magazine exploded.

As Troy swung Stingray sharply away, the shock waves caught it, hurling it towards the wall of the canyon.

His face grim, he fought to get control of the vessel. He saw the dark wall loom up in the searchlights and brought the nose up and round, but a second shock wave struck it, flinging it sideways like a scrap of paper in a wind. He felt a jolt as the port stabilizer fin grazed the wall. For a brief instant Stingray seemed to stall, and then sped on in a wide upward arc.

"Terror fish number three!" Phones proclaimed. "Right on our tail!"

"They usually hunt in packs," Troy growled. "Stand by! Rate six!"

He flung Stingray into another steep climb, but something was wrong. It veered sharply to port as if the starboard booster had too much thrust. It took all his skill to stop the vessel from crashing into the rock face. Sweat broke out on his brow as he got it away by the skin of his teeth.

He glanced at the instrument bank. The speedometer needle was barely registering five hundred knots instead of six. Something was wrong all right. The port booster must be out of action. He cut the starboard booster.

"Look out, Troy!"

He saw that the terror fish was swinging, coming round to the attack again. His throat tightened when he realised that Stingray was dead in line with its sights.

"Hold on!" he cried as he flung the super sub into a crash dive. His warning was all that saved Marina from being slammed across the cabin with spine shattering force. The Titan missile sped through Stingray's jet thrust and hurtled on through the dark water to explode harmlessly down the canyon.

As the terror fish flashed past overhead, Troy levelled out a few feet above the canyon floor, the powerful jets stirring up the silt of ages into a dense grey-white fog.

Climbing sharply through the murk, he saw the Titan craft turning. He knew he no longer had the edge on it for speed now his boosters were not working. Relentlessly he drove up at it, getting it dead in his sights.

"Fire port sting missile!" he ordered.

Once again a slim torpedo hissed from its tube and struck home with deadly force, and the third of Titan's killer squadron followed the others into flaming oblivion.

As the white-hot debris drifted down into the ooze, Troy spiralled up, searchlights probing the darkness, scanners working, seeking more lurking enemies.

He levelled off at five thousand feet and pushed his cap back to mop his brow. "We sure had some narrow squeaks."

"What were those sea lizards doing this far south?" Phones growled.

"Titan's got mines most places. But that net showed they were aiming to snare us if they could."

"Yeah. Standing orders, I reckon—catch us or destroy us. Titan couldn't have known we were heading this way, Troy."

"Guess not. What happened to that port booster, Phones?"

Phones was checking his instruments. "It's out of action. Nothing registering. Must have happened when we grazed the cliff face. Looks like a repair job. Do we stop and fix it?"

"No, we'll carry on till we locate the position of that marker buoy. That signal still coming through?"

"Yeah, but it's kind of faint."

"Just our luck if its battery cell's failing. Let's get cracking. Rate four. That's the highest we can do now, I guess."

* * *

Twenty miles later they emerged into the main trench and Phones reported three thousand fathoms below them.

But the signal from the buoy was even fainter, and an hour later it had faded altogether, although they were over four hundred miles nearer.

"What now?" Phones asked.

We'll take a chance on that original reading of yours, Phones, and split the difference at seven-fifty miles from where you first picked up the signal. A cruising radius of a hundred miles should cover the vital area."

"That means we've got about another three-fifty miles to go, Troy."

* * *

Less than an hour later, after carefully reconnoitring through the videoscan periscope, they surfaced on the blue-green, wind-whipped ocean within sight of the Peruvian coast.

Far to the west, across the heaving waste, the sun was low in the pearly sky. In another three hours, it would plunge into the sea and night would come with tropical suddenness.

Troy mounted into the conning tower and surveyed the shoreline through powerful binoculars.

A few miles to the south of their position was a small town of white buildings, with a shoal of small coastal craft close in-shore. At a quay, a few ocean-going tramps were moored. It looked like a mining town.

Beyond the foam-edged beaches, the coastal desert strip stretched away, bare and glistening yellow, to the dark foothills of the Andes, which reared their snowy peaks through banks of cloud.

All along the coast, vast flocks of birds– white, brown and grey– wheeled and screeched and dived for fish. Gulls and terns and pelicans and guanays—the guano birds that contributed wealth to Peru in the form of islands of rich manure.

A little to the north of the town, low rocky headlands enclosed a small secluded bay.

Troy studied it for a few moments, then, after sweeping the ocean all round in a vain attempt to sight the now silent buoy, he descended into the cabin again.

"Guess that town must be Hatica," he said, consulting a map of the Peruvian coastline. "A couple of miles north there's a small bay and the charts say there's a deep water channel into it. We'll put it there and repair that port booster. No one's likely to spot us."

"Does it matter?" Phones asked.

"It could. If Hagen's in this area and the news got around that a WASP vessel had turned up he wouldn't think it was a coincidence."

"Guess not."

They submerged and slowly entered the little bay. There was deep water right up to the low cliff, with a convenient overhang to hide Stingray in the unlikely event of anyone coming along the arid featureless shoreline.

Sea birds whirled about them, screeching and diving for fish and fighting over the spoils.

Troy and Phones put on swim gear and went out to examine the damaged booster unit. It was beyond repair, and that meant fitting one of the spares they carried.

In the WASP repair shop at Marineville, the task might have taken half an hour. The sun was almost down by the time Troy and Phones were through.

"What now?" asked Phones, as they took off their swim gear and sat down to a hasty meal in the standby lounge.

"Locating that buoy's not going to be easy, Phones," said Troy thoughtfully. "If it's not radiating, it'll be a daylight chore. But if Hagen's up to something off this part of the coast someone may know about it."

Phones looked at him shrewdly.

"You thinking we might take a trip into Hatica and make a few inquiries?"

"That was the idea," Troy said. "But I'm going alone. You stay with Stingray, Phones."

"Now, look here, Troy   —"

"Quit arguing, Phones. It's an order."

"Some guys get all the fun," Phones said disgustedly.

"I'm not aiming to run into trouble, Phones. If that's what you're thinking."

"Maybe, but you'll find it," Phones said resignedly. "You always do, or maybe it just comes looking for you. Better take a couple of distress rockets."

Troy chuckled and changed into old slacks, a shirt and jacket which he always kept in the wardroom locker for use on occasions like this. As darkness spread swiftly over the land, he went ashore aboard a monocopter.

* * *

He kept to the edge of the water. The sand was firmer here than in the desert strip. All was quiet now that the screeching birds had settled down for the night, but he could see the white flocks floating on the water like clouds against a dark sky. Over the mountains the moon was coming up, touching the snow of the peaks with silver.

Presently the lights on a masthead came into sight.

As he reached the little harbour on foot, a fishing boat with an outboard motor went chugging out through the wide sand-choked entrance. The man at the tiller was singing a mournful song in a tuneless, warbling voice.

From the town came the faint blare of music.

He made his way along the quay. Below he saw a cigarette glow in the dark. A man who had just come ashore in a small launch was mooring it at the foot of some steps.

Troy waited in the shadows. Who better to ask about Hagen than a man who made his livelihood from the sea?

The man left the boat and slowly climbed the steps, taking off his floppy panama to cuff his brow.

Troy moved forward casually.

And then the man passed under the lamp that hung from a warehouse wall and the light fell upon his face.

Troy caught his breath and stepped back quickly into the shadows again. For the man was José, whom he had last seen on the Santa Anna.

Chapter Five
TROUBLE FOR TROY

José left the wharf and slouched up an alley towards the lighted town. Keeping to the deeper shadows, Troy stalked him silently.

José had come ashore in a launch, so Hagen could not be so very far away. But why had the man come to this small and shabby town on the edge of beyond? For stores? There should have been enough in the vessel Hagen had stolen to last him for months.

Troy considered grabbing José and trying to force him to reveal where Number Thirteen was but that plan had its difficulties. If José managed to get away he'd be able to warn Hagen that someone was on his trail, and that was the last thing Troy wanted right then, for Atlanta's sake.

He told himself it would be better to follow José and find out what his business was in Hatica. Afterwards— well, maybe somehow he could trail José back to Number Thirteen.

The alley led into a wide main street ankle-deep in sand that looked a dirty yellow in the dim lights strung from concrete posts at intervals along one side, where the prevailing wind had piled the sand in drifts feet high.

The buildings were mostly single storey adobes, thatched with reeds or roofed with corrugated iron. Here and there a two-storey concrete building reared its squat shape, and on the fringe of the desert beyond rose the huge kilns and derricks of a sulphur mine that was probably Hatica's main source of income and employment.

The town looked like something out of the past or from a movie set. It could have changed little in the last hundred years or so.

José was moving slowly along the side of the street without lamps, his white clothing just visible in the shadows.

Troy eased out of the alley and followed.

The moon was above the mountains now, adding its faint light to the scene. The smell of cooking mingled with the acrid tang of sulphur. Heat-drenched sand and adobe bricks released the warmth from the day into the night air.

Further up the street, a small group of men ambled from the shadows on one side into the shadows on the other. A dog howled and others chorused an answer.

Troy steadily gained on José, his feet making a mere whisper of sound in the sand. Troy was only ten yards from him when he stopped outside a seedy-looking cantina and looked warily about.

Troy melted into the deeper shadows of a storefront and stood there, tense. Had José suspected he was being followed?

Then the other man stepped onto the cafe porch and thrust open the door. A narrow shaft of yellow light stabbed out. A murmur of voices and the faint strumming of a guitar mingled with a sorrowful voice flowed out in a low wash of sound. Then light and sound were abruptly cut off again as the door swung to after José.

Troy cat-footed to the porch and, hugging the wall to the right of it, peered through the grimy window.

The cantina was crowded. Mostly the customers were locals or descendants of the Mayan and Incan tribes from the mountains. However, some American oil workers were playing poker at a table by themselves.

Troy registered these details briefly in his mind as he looked for José.

He, at last, spotted him at the rear of the smoke-wreathed room, standing beside a table, talking to three men as lean and rapacious-looking as himself.

Troy stood there, uncertain about his next move. To follow José into the cantina would be to invite attention to himself. He was a stranger in a town which probably saw few strangers, especially after sundown. The very fact that José had attracted little attention seemed to indicate he was fairly well-known here.

But, as he hesitated, he saw the three men rise, pick up their glasses and bottles, and follow José through a bead-curtained doorway at the rear of the room.

Troy spun away and slipped down the narrow alley at the side of the cantina to a back lot deep in sand and stinking of garbage.

To one side of a rear door was a steamed-up window— the kitchen, he thought. On the other side was a smaller window over which tattered curtains were drawn.

Troy, peering in through the curtained window, got a glimpse of José tossing down a drink. The South American put down the glass and then began speaking forcefully to someone Troy could not see. Troy could hear the murmur of voices but could distinguish no words.

He stepped back, looking up at the roof in the moonlight. It was flat and of reed thatch. At the corner of the building stood a rainwater barrel. Troy reckoned it rained in Hatica every other blue moon, but when it did rain, every drop was precious.

He climbed on the barrel. It was empty and sun-warped and creaked ominously under his weight. He balanced himself gingerly on the rim, reached up and over the edge of the roof and got a firm grip on the osier binding of the thatch.

Just as he was about to haul himself onto the roof, the rear door of the cantina opened and a man in a white apron came out with a bucket.

Troy froze, his heart pounding. For a few agonizing moments, he stood there, the barrel protesting under him. But its sound was smothered by the clatter of cutlery and plates which came from the kitchen, and the man threw out some garbage from the bucket, then went back inside without so much as a glance in his direction.

Gradually, Troy eased himself up onto the roof. Spread-eagled there, he listened. He could hear José's voice, but still he could not distinguish clearly what he was saying.

There was a narrow sliver of light coming from a little gap in the thatch. He thrust his hand into it gently, worked it about cautiously until he had widened the gap sufficiently for him to peer down into the room below.

He saw José standing with his back to the closed door of a little room, talking earnestly with a wealth of gestures to the other three men, who were sitting at a table, glasses in hand, regarding him doubtfully, almost suspiciously.

José was speaking in Spanish, but it was a language Troy understood well.

"The hombre will pay you in good American dollars, amigos," José said. "Gold if you wish it."

"How many dollars?" demanded one of the men flatly.

"A thousand. Is it not good pay, amigos, for maybe only a few days' work?"

"A thousand dollars to us," said another of the men, a dark-faced ruffian with a broken nose and fierce black eyebrows. "But how much will you forget to take out of your pocket when you pay us, José?"

Then José drew himself up with an air of injured dignity.

"Carlos!" he exclaimed in a shocked tone. "You insult me. You think that I, José Arrientos Mendoza, would stoop to a mean thing like that, cheating an amigo?"

"Si, si, I think that! I think you would cheat your own blind grandmother out of her last grain of maize, José." Carlos's right hand flashed up to his neck and a wicked-bladed throwing knife seemed to leap into his hand. He smiled savagely as he pointed it at José. "How much did the hombre tell you to offer us, amigo?"

José licked his lips and smiled nervously. "How much? I think perhaps my memory was bad a moment ago, Carlos. It is the fault of travelling so long underwater."

"How much?" Carlos cut in impatiently, his lean dark fingers playing with the carved haft of the knife.

"Er—fifteen hundred dollars, amigo," José said hastily.

"Caramba! Now you talk our language!" Carlos laughed harshly and stroked the knife almost lovingly as he slid it into the neck sheath under his loosely knotted bandanna. "My little Maria, she is a good memory tickler, si? Perhaps we take on this job for the Americano."

"Wait!" said the third man, who had not yet spoken. "This Americano—what is he, José? Why does he want us to work for him?"

José smiled slyly. "Professor Hagen is a famous man, an archaeologist, Santos. He explores the ocean looking for things from the past, like cities the sea has swallowed."

"And so he will pay us fifteen hundred dollars each to do some diving for him?" asked Santos with a thin smile. "Perhaps he is what the Americanos call the screwball —a loco hombre, si?"

José shrugged. "He does not seem crazy to me, amigos. I think he is a very rich hombre. The money—poof! It means nothing to him!"

"Bueno!" Carlos grinned. "Then maybe he will give us two thousand dollars each, huh?"

"Maybe," José said.

But he said it in a way that convinced Troy that two thousand was more likely the actual sum Hagen had told him to offer these three cut-throats.

"It is worth two thousand," Santos said seriously. "Those waters are difficult to work in."

He broke off, looking up sharply at the ceiling as the thatch stirred under Troy's weight and a few seed husks drifted down.

"What was that?" he demanded suspiciously.

The others looked up and Troy held his breath. He was sure José's eyes were fixed on his through the hole he had made in the thatch.

"It is nothing," Carlos growled. "The rats hide in the reeds waiting for the lights to go out so they can raid the kitchen."

The third man drew their minds back to what they had been discussing. "It is not only the waters that are difficult. There is El Monstruo!"

"El Monstruo?" Carlos sneered at him. "That is just a fairy story invented by the old women to scare the babies, Lopez. No one has ever seen him."

"How do we know?" insisted Lopez, scowling. "Maybe those who see him never return to tell of it."

"There is no need to worry about El Monstruo," José assured them with a smile. "Professor Hagen has powerful weapons that will deal with any monster of the deeps, amigos."

"So! Your Americano has powerful weapons too?" Carlos said softly. "He is just a peaceful man of science, but he carries powerful weapons. I am becoming very interested in your Americano. Tell me, José, why does he not come to Hatica himself to look for divers instead of sending you alone at night?"

José spread his claw-like hands. "You do not understand these Americanos, amigo. Always they are jealous of each other. Professor Hagen is afraid that perhaps his rivals hear he is hiring divers and they come to see what he is doing and find what he is looking for first."

Carlos shook his head in mock disapproval. "These gringos, they are so dishonest." He leered. "But I think maybe the professor will pay more than two thousand dollars with a little persuasion, huh?"

"Maybe," said José, with a cunning smile. "But we must not kill the goose that lays the egg of gold, Carlos. There are other ways…"

He lowered his voice, and, although Troy pressed his ear to the hole in the thatch, he could not hear what José was saying.

When José had finished, Carlos laughed savagely and slapped his hand on the table, "It is a good idea, amigo. My thoughts were already drifting in that direction. But just where would we have to dive?"

"I have a map," José said, taking a piece of paper from the pocket of his grubby white jacket and spreading it out on the table before the three men.

They leaned forward eagerly, obstructing Troy's view of it, and he edged himself forward along the thatch, seeking a gap through which he could see it.

Without warning the tinder-dry reeds beneath him gave way and he plunged down into the room headfirst.

As the men below flung themselves back from the table with startled yells, Troy crashed down on it, shoulder twisted to take the shock. The table disintegrated into matchwood under his weight.

Troy's trained reactions were quicker than theirs. While they stood flabbergasted, he rolled over, snatched up one of the legs of the smashed table and flung it at the solitary old-fashioned electric light bulb hanging from a beam above him. His aim was true and the bulb exploded into a thousand fragments. Darkness blanketed the room, relieved only by the faint moonlight filtering through the window.

"A spy!" It was Carlos who snarled. "Get him, amigos!"

Troy saw the dim silhouette of someone hurtling at him. He rolled quickly in that direction and the lunging man tripped over him and fell headlong. He heard the tinkle of a falling knife.

As he scrambled to his feet, another figure loomed up. He sensed rather than saw the upraised knife-hand and lashed out with his fist. He felt it crunch home on a nose, and with a gasp of pain, the man staggered back and went down with a crash.

A hand clawed at Troy's leg. He kicked out and felt his foot sink into yielding flesh. There was a grunt in the darkness and the hand fell away.

Something whistled past his head and he felt the knife blade's mark searing along his cheek. As his assailant's arm came down hard on his shoulder with the force of the stabbing blow, Troy grabbed the sinewy wrist, jerked forward and swung. With a screech of terror and agony, the man went flying over his head to thud against the adobe wall and subside with a low moan.

Troy's cheek was smarting. He could feel the hot blood trickling down. He knew this unequal fight in the dark could not last long. His luck must soon run out. His only advantage was that he knew everyone else was an enemy, whereas they couldn't be sure who was who.

It was time to get out—fast.

Already someone was hammering on the door leading from the cantina, which apparently José had locked.

Troy saw the moonlit square of the window a few yards from him. He charged for it. A hand grabbed him and he thrust his shoulder hard into the man's chest, sending him reeling away.

Then, shielding his head with his arms, he took a running dive through the window, carrying glass and frame with him. He landed on his shoulder in the deep sand of the back lot, rolling to take the shock of the fall.

Instinct, born of living so long with danger, made him keep on rolling, and he thanked his stars when he heard the crack of a gun and felt the sting of sand in his face as the bullet whipped through the spot where he had lain an instant before.

But in the moonlight, he was still an easy target. Even as the kitchen door was flung open, he scrambled to his feet and hared off through the backlots towards the waterfront.

Shots tattooed their message of hate, but the aim was wild and none of the bullets came close enough to his racing figure to be dangerous.

But already the pursuit was on. Glancing back as he dashed into an alley, he saw a pack of them tearing after him. That backward glance was deadly. A discarded box tripped him and he went down to plough the dust with his face. Winded by the crash, he forced himself to his feet and staggered on. He could see the gleam of the moonlight on the water ahead now, at the end of the alley.

Something whistled close to his head and clattered against a wall. That was Carlos, he thought with a gulp. A right handy guy with a knife, the most to be feared of the four ruffians on whom he had snooped.

He came out on the quayside. He didn't hesitate but dived straight in. The cold water revived his flagging strength and he kept under, swimming as fast as he could towards the harbour entrance.

But presently he was forced to come up for air. He saw figures racing along the quay.

"After him!" yelled a voice he thought was José's. "I've got a launch, amigos!"

Troy looked about him desperately. He had no chance of beating that launch to the harbour entrance, especially if it had a searchlight beam. A pale patch between him and the harbour wall caught his eye, and his heart leapt. There was just one slender chance.

Gulping down air into his lungs, he dived again and, when he surfaced once more, he was only a few yards from the pale patch, and found he had rightly guessed it was a flock of sleeping gulls. If they were aware of his nearness, they gave no sign of it.

He heard a powerful motor roar into life and knew José had started the launch. He dived deeply and a moment or so later surfaced as silently as he could in the middle of the gulls and hung there treading water.

He watched anxiously as the white shape of the launch swung round the harbour and came towards the gulls. If it scared them away he would have to take another dive. But the birds were used to the coming and going of motorboats and did not move. The launch turned away, skirting the edge of the flock and then taking a spiralling course back to the quay.

He could see José at the wheel, while Carlos was leaning over the bows shining a powerful torch on the placid surface of the dark water.

Troy grunted his relief and then took another deep breath and dived again, swimming on towards the harbour entrance. He planned to scramble ashore beyond the harbour and make his way along the sands to the adjoining inlet where Stingray lay.

He surfaced in the rougher water of the harbour entrance and pushed ahead. Suddenly he missed a stroke and floundered, his heart thudding. Cutting through the water ahead was the sinister triangular fin of a shark.

Maybe it had scented the blood that was still oozing from his knifed cheek. He could never reach the shore in time.

His reactions were instinctive rather than consciously triggered by his brain. Drawing the knife from his belt sheath, he dived, straight towards the marauder of the depths, dived deep enough to get beneath it, while its own momentum carried it on above him.

He saw its huge shape silhouetted against the moonlit water, saw the cruel gash of its mouth and the pallid underside.

Even as it sensed him and swung, he struck upwards with all his strength. He felt razor-sharp teeth slash his left arm, but the knife sank home, deep into a vital spot.

In a frenzy of pain, the creature thrashed away, taking the knife with it, and vanished into the darkness.

Troy struggled to the surface, gulping greedily at the night air. He was outside the harbour now, in deep water. He was conscious of a strong current plucking at him. He tried to swim towards the headland beyond which Stingray lay, but his left arm was numb and useless. The relentless current tugged at him, dragging him out into the open ocean.

He thought vaguely of the wounded shark, its lifeblood draining away into the sea to lay a trail that would bring others of its kind racing to devour it. And when it was gone, they would scent him.

Out of the corner of his eye, he saw a dim shape gliding through the water towards him. Already? With the last of his strength, he tried to change course to swim away from it, even though his fuddled mind told him it was useless.

And then suddenly blackness seemed to engulf him and he knew no more as he spun down into merciful oblivion.

Chapter Six
LEGEND OF THE DEEP

Troy didn't know how long he was unconscious, but when he came round he was surprised to find himself staring up at the moonlit sky. There was a gentle rocking motion beneath him and gradually it dawned on him that he was lying in a small boat.

His first thought was that he had been captured by José and his friends. He started up, but a wave of nausea lashed him and he sank back with a faint groan.

Someone moved in the boat behind his head, then a figure in a baggy white jacket and shapeless panama loomed above him. A dark, wrinkled face stared down at him.

"Hola Senor." said the man in halting English. "Medicine muy bien. Have some more."

The man squatted beside him and raised him into a sitting position, pouring an evil-tasting concoction into his mouth from a tin beaker.

Troy swallowed and grimaced. "Thanks," he said, forcing a grin.

Black, beady eyes studied him solemnly from the wizened mask of a face.

"It is a traditional drink for war wound. My people brew this medicine from the time of Inca. Power to heal the arm, si?"

Troy remembered his encounter with the shark then and glanced down at his left arm. It was bandaged neatly, and although it was throbbing faintly, there was no real pain in it. The drug must be a mild herbal remedy that allayed hunger pains and sped recovery. It certainly seemed to have worked wonders on his arm.

He grinned up at the man. "Thanks, mister! Sure was swell of you to save me from the sharks. I'd given myself up for lost."

"I fish when I see you. You are lucky. Tonight I fish close to shore." The man paused, then went on, "Men come in motorboat, looking for you."

"They did? You know the guys?"

"Ugh! One called Carlos. Know him. Another José— not see before. They ask about amigo who swim from Hatica. Not see you under nets. Bad hombres."

"Well, I'm not going to argue about that, mister. What do I call you, anyway?"

"Manco."

"I'm mighty grateful to you, Manco. First, you save me from sea sharks, then from land sharks——"

Troy broke off. From somewhere in the darkness had come a low menacing rumble like distant thunder. Suddenly the sea beneath the boat heaved up as if a whale had surfaced under it. He fell back into the bottom of the boat and for a moment it seemed to be suspended there between water and starry sky. Then it flopped back into a trough, shipping a little water.

A moment later the sea was calm again, and the little boat was riding smoothly on the gentle phosphorescent swell.

"What in the name of Neptune was that?" Troy gasped, sitting up and staring at Manco, who squatted unperturbed through the brief but startling upheaval.

"The earth shakes itself."

"Huh?" Then light dawned on Troy. "You mean it was an earth tremor, Manco?"

"Always they happen here. No one takes notice."

Troy remembered this was one of the great earthquake zones of the world. It was from here that some of the most disastrous tsunamis had originated. Without warning, a submarine earthquake would set in motion on the surface of the Pacific a vast wave which would race across the ocean to the shores of mainland and island nations alike, rising higher and higher until it was a huge wall of water perhaps eighty feet high and travelling at four hundred knots. Nothing could withstand it, although for the last century efficient early warning systems had prevented thousands of lives from being lost in those terror waves.

"Where you want to go?" Manco asked, going back to his outboard motor. "You not Hatica hombre, so not take you there."

Although Troy was grateful to the old man for saving his life, he did not intend to take him into his confidence. No one must know who he was or why he was here until he was sure Atlanta was safe.

He glanced at the lights of the town off the starboard, getting his bearings, then pointed to a headland about half a mile distant.

"Guess I'll be okay if you put me ashore on that headland, Manco."

The fisherman displayed no curiosity, but started the motor and sat stolidly at the tiller as the boat crept steadily towards the headland.

"Many times earth shakes itself because it is angry," Manco said as if resuming the conversation they'd been having before he asked Troy where he wanted to be put ashore.

"Four or five hundred years ago it was very angry. When Spanish men come to this island they build big city south of Hatica. Big cathedral. Many houses. Many ships come and take away silver. Spanish men make my people dig in mines at Potosi."

"Potosi? Sure, I've heard of that, Manco. Go on! What happened?"

"One night the earth was very angry because so much of its wealth was taken away. So it shakes itself, like the dog that has been in the water. Next morning the big city is not there."

"No? Where was it?"

Manco gestured over the side.

"It vanish down there, senor. No one ever see it again. But sometimes when all is quiet, perhaps you hear the bells of cathedral."

Troy paused, and listened to the night as if expecting to hear ringing on the wind. "You ever heard 'em, Manco?"

"I think. Not sure. My father hear them. Not good to hear them. Something bad happen."

Troy grinned into the darkness as the boat grounded on the headland beach. Similar legends existed everywhere in the world. But then he remembered something he had overheard in that room at the back of the cantina before he'd unintentionally dropped in on José and his pals.

"Ever heard of El Monstruo?" he asked Manco as he stepped ashore.

Manco's didn't answer at first. Slowly, he nodded. His face was expressionless.

"Ever seen it?"

"People who see it do not live to tell about it, senor."

That was what Lopez had suggested, Troy reminded himself.

"Any idea what it is?" he asked.

"No, senor. But there is a story…"

"Yeah?"

"It guards the way to treasures of Sanito."

"Sanito?"

"City the earth shake under sea, senor."

Manco pushed off his boat and drifted away into the night.

Troy stood there staring after the boat until the darkness had swallowed it and only the faint chugging of the outboard motor and the swishing of the breakers disturbed the stillness.

Did Manco know more than he was prepared to tell?

As Troy crunched his way around the beach to the low cliff beneath which Stingray lay concealed his pulse quickened with excitement.

He was sure it was no coincidence that Conrad Hagen had brought Number Thirteen here, to Hatica where there was a legend of a lost treasure city beneath the waves.

"Hold it, mister!" a voice growled.

A figure stepped from the rock shadows and Troy saw the glint of moonlight on gunmetal.

He chuckled softly. "Okay! Don't shoot! I'll come quietly!"

"Troy!"

Phones came forward eagerly. He was dressed as roughly as Troy was.

"Gee, pal," he said in a relieved voice, "I was just on my way to look for you. I figured you'd run into bad trouble."

"I hit trouble all right, Phones. But I guess it was good trouble for us. Tell you about it when we're aboard. You ought to be court-martialed for disobeying orders to stay put," Troy's tone took on mock severity as they picked their way over the rocks.

"Yeah?" snorted Phones. "Well, somewhere in regulations there's a clause that says a crew can take over from the skipper if they think he's nuts, and seeing Marina and me are unanimous about that——"

"Okay, buddy!" Troy chuckled. "I cry quits."

* * *

Marina's lovely face fit up with relief when Troy followed Phones down into the control cabin. But when she saw his bandaged arm and knife-scratched cheek, concern showed in her sea-green eyes.

Mutely, she insisted on examining the wounds while Troy began his story and Phones took Stingray out to sea and submerged it to fifty fathoms.

Marina smiled approval when she saw the condition of the wound on Troy's arm, but before she re-dressed it she used a special shark wound salve known to the peoples of the ocean depths.

When Troy had finished, Phones frowned.

"It sure puts us in the picture, Troy. Guess you must be right about Hagen being around here someplace. But I can't see a guy like that falling for a deep-sea treasure yarn. They're as common as seashells, but not one in a thousand's got any truth in it."

"This could be number one-thousand-and-one," Troy argued. "Maybe Hagen's got a pretty good notion where to start looking—that's why he wants those hoodlums for divers. Anyway, the great thing is we know roughly where to cast our own dragnet. Let's get cracking."

"What if José recognised you when you dropped in on their little tea party?" Phones asked after Troy had taken over the controls and swung Stingray southwards parallel with the coast.

"Million to one chance. I had that light out before they knew that had happened, and José wouldn't have known me anyway in those old clothes, I reckon."

"Maybe. But he'll report to Hagen someone was snooping."

"Sure, but I figure Hagen will reckon it's some rival crook trying to horn in on his prospect. He'll be on the lookout for trouble. We'll go deep, Phones. Won't be so easy for his scanners to pick us up."

Slowly they descended. One thousand feet... two thousand... three... Down... down... down... Eight thousand.

For hundreds of fathoms, the only sign of life they'd seen had been a few rat-tails and small deep sea squids, but the sound scans were bringing in hoots, grunts, whistles, and whisperings from distant creatures.

Troy hadn't switched on the searchlights but the cabin lights showed that the water outside was crystal clear.

Ten thousand feet... twelve...

They were well down in the trench now, although the echo sounders showed there was as much water again below them.

Far down in the hadal depths at the bottom of the great trench, Stingray would probably be safe from detection but such a tremendous depth created its own problems. Stingray was a twenty-first century marvel of submarine engineering built to resist pressures of tens of thousands of tons. But the little two-man aquasprites used for reconnaissance could not operate with complete safety so far down. Neither could a human, even equipped with special high helium content air supplies to give resistance to the pressure.

Anyway, Troy reasoned, four miles down was too far. Even if by some improbable chance a city like the legendary Sanito had sunk so far, the pressure would have flattened it and made it impossible to explore. If it did exist, it was nearer the surface, much nearer even than Stingray's present depth.

He levelled off and cruised on, hugging the port wall of the great trench, the one nearer the continental slope down which the forgotten city must have slipped. If it had slipped at all.

Mile after mile disappeared into the black void behind them, but nothing registered except the monotonous pinging of the port scanner keeping them at a safe distance from the sheer rock wall.

In vain, Phones manipulated the sensitive controls, seeking the distinctive note that would indicate another underwater craft somewhere ahead or above them.

Twenty miles south of Hatica the port scanner's graph traced a deep ledge with an overhang.

"We'll park here," he told Phones. "That overhang will screen Stingray while we reconnoitre."

Skilfully, they steered the super sub over the ledge and beneath the overhang. It settled gently on its skids and the cabin lights, softly humming motors and pinging scanners were switched off.

The noises of the distant sea creatures coming over the hydrophone speakers were the only sounds that broke the cold, abyssal silence that settled about the submarine.

"I'll take Marina," Troy said decisively, unstrapping himself from his seat.

"But Troy!" Phones protested. "Marina can look after Stingray as well as I can!"

"Sure, but you can't swim in the dark the way she can. Sorry, Phones, but I'll need her as a guide. We shan't be able to risk torches."

Phones regarded him scornfully. "You sure have got an answer for everything, pal. Sure, it wouldn't occur to you that you're not one hundred per cent fit for swim patrol with that wounded arm?"

"Find that in the regulations, lieutenant, and I'll back down and detail you for the chore," Troy grinned, standing up and flexing his limbs.

"I said you had an answer for everything!" Phones muttered in disgust.

Troy changed into his underwater gear. Marina needed no such aid to swim in the depths, where she was as much at home as any of Titan's aquaphibians. Troy was always amazed at her refusal to wear any protection, despite incredible pressures and temperatures. "One of these days we're going to have to bring you into the Doc for an exam!" he said, shaking his head. "You're a wonder of nature."

Before they entered the airlock, Troy said, "We won't contact you unless it's a number one emergency, Phones. If Hagen picks up our voice, even if we talk in code, he'll know someone's on his tail. We've got to keep him guessing as long as we can."

"Okay. But if you aren't back in two hours, I'm coming to look for you, pal."

Troy nodded. "That's a reasonable margin. We should be able to reconnoitre three or four miles of this rock wall in that time. Be seeing you."

Marina led the way from the airlock and swam gracefully above the ledge in the direction Stingray had been travelling, her long hair floating out behind her in the faint light from the instrument panels in the control cabin.

When that light faded, Troy was relieved to see there was a faint luminescence shining from microscopic algae-like growths on the rock wall. It gave sufficient light for him to follow Marina's twinkling bare feet as she sped through the dark water ahead of him.

The ledge continued at roughly the same level for several hundred yards and then began to rise steeply like a path carved up a sloping canyon wall.

Marina paused, treading water, glancing back at him as if for instructions. He motioned her to follow the ledge upwards and she swam on.

There was no vegetable growth this far down where the sun's rays never penetrated. But there was life of a sort apart from the occasional electric fish that darted past and the microscopic luminescent growths that clung to the rock wall.

Troy saw clusters of enormous sea anemones. They contracted their waving tentacles into jelly bodies as they sensed Marina's approach.

There were brittle stars too, and once a shoal of shrimps swam over him, brushing the exposed brow above his face mask with feathery antennae.

He became conscious of a dull ache in his wounded arm, and he felt he was tiring more quickly than usual. He glanced at the luminous face of his wrist chronometer and was surprised to find it was almost half an hour since they had left Stingray. The built-in depth gauge registered just over ten thousand feet, so they were climbing pretty rapidly.

Suddenly, he realised that Marina had stopped again and was signalling urgently to him, motioning towards the rock wall. She had seen something ahead or sensed it as fish sense vibrations warning them of the approach of prey or enemies.

He swam close to the wall and forced himself down flat on the ledge, holding himself there by jamming his fingers into a tiny crevice. He got a glimpse of Marina fading from sight a few yards ahead of him, and then suddenly he saw what had alarmed her.

Coming through the darkness was a faint glow. At first, he thought it was some large luminescent sea creature, but as it drew nearer, he saw it was the headlamp of an aquasprite.

His pulses quickened. The hunch he had been playing all along had paid off. That aquasprite could only have come from the stolen Number Thirteen.

He hugged the ledge as it slowly approached. He saw it was following the line of the ledge, and the headlamp was playing on it as if the crew were seeking something.

Surely they could not have learned somehow that he and Marina were on it?

He put his head between his extended arms so that nothing of the pale skin of his face could show in the light of the beam. His swim gear would be inconspicuous against the dark rock.

He took a deep breath and held it so that no bubbles would betray him. The light came nearer. He wondered if Marina was visible. She would have the savvy to hide her face and her long hair would look like some marine growth, he told himself.

The light swam over him, sweeping down between his screening arms and reflecting into his eyes from the rock below, dazzling him slightly.

Maybe it was his imagination, but it seemed to hover there for an eternity, while his lungs came near to bursting and his ears began to sing.

And then it was going on, plunging him into blessed darkness again, and he let his stale breath out in a long sigh.

He glanced round. The 'sprite was going on down the wall, following the slope of the ledge and playing its beam on it still. If it followed the ledge far enough, the crew must see Stingray.

In a moment of sheer panic, he raised his hand to switch on his hydrophone transmitter to warn Phones but realised in moments the foolishness of it. He would only succeed in warning the men in the 'sprite, too. Phone's sensitive instruments would pick up the little craft long before Stingray was within range of its own less powerful scanners, and Phones would take evasive action.

But even as the thought went through his mind, he saw to his relief that the aquasprite was rising above the level of the ledge, was going up almost vertically, and was playing its beam on the sloping cliff face. Gradually, it faded from his sight into the blackness of the waters above.

He lay there for a moment, letting the tension drain out of him and waiting for Marina to swim back to him.

But she didn't come. A vague fear began to gnaw at him.

Pushing himself off, he swam up to the spot where he thought he had seen her dive for cover. In the faint luminescence, he saw a crevice. The dark slash in the rock wall was scarcely big enough to admit him.

He realised she must have dived inside to avoid being seen by the men in the aquasprite. But why didn't she come out again? What had happened to her?

That fear grew, knifing into him. He switched on his headlamp and squeezed into the crevice. In his anxiety for her, he stopped caring whether the light might be seen by any other men of Hagen on the prowl in Number Thirteen's second 'sprite.

The crevice widened into a shallow cavern, the floor of which was silted and littered with small rocks. At first, he saw nothing more, but as he turned his head to the right the light beam played on what looked like a mass of writhing green snakes as thick as his arm. Beyond it was a squat trunk of wine-coloured jelly fastened to the rock wall.

An icy hand seemed to squeeze his heart. The thing was a monstrous sea anemone, and in the middle of its writhing tentacles was the limp figure of Marina!

Slowly, relentlessly, the giant tentacles were dragging the unconscious girl headfirst towards a cavernous, toothless mouth that yawned at the top of that huge gelatinous body.

With a harsh cry of mingled horror and loathing, Troy snatched his knife from his belt and plunged at the monstrous creature.

A tentacle whipped out at him and he felt a fiery stinging sensation on his exposed forehead as if he had fallen headlong into a bed of giant nettles.

He struck out viciously, severing the writhing thing with one sweep of his razor-sharp blade.

Marina's head was perilously near that hideous fleshy-lipped mouth.

He knew the anemone was a mindless thing, a voracious feeder by instinct on anything that strayed within reach of its hundreds of sensitive tentacles, but that without them it was powerless.

In desperate determination, he slashed again and again at the tentacles which writhed about Marina. At first, he seemed to make no impression. Always there seemed to be another ready to take the place of the one he hacked off.

Then, suddenly, the remaining tentacles retracted, vanishing into the vast mouth, which closed on them, leaving only a pulsating mass of red jelly anchored to the rock wall. The still faintly writhing tentacles he had severed drifted slowly away into the darkness.

Marina was floating motionless in the water. After a quick glance round in the light of his headbeam to make sure there were no other lurking dangers, Troy swam to her.

Big white blistering swellings on her face, throat and hands showed that the anemone's paralysing poison had been unleashed. Unprotected by swim gear as he was, she had fallen easy prey to it when she had dived into the crevice.

Troy knew that every moment she remained in the coma added to her danger. WASP swim gear was provided with a first-aid kit for emergencies like this. He took out the special hypodermic, ready charged with a heart stimulant, and carefully injected it.

Anxious seconds ticked away, and then he let out a great sigh of relief when he saw her eyelids flicker open.

"Come on," he said when she was fully recovered. "We'd better get back to Stingray."

She nodded, smiling.

Then suddenly the smile went from her blistered face and she caught his arm in agitation.

"What's the matter, Marina? You heard something?"

But before she could reply he heard it himself. A deep rumbling welled up into his headphones until it became an ear-splitting roar.

In that same instant, the water in the cave became violently agitated.

"Earth tremor!" he yelled, grabbing her hand. "Let's get out of here into open water."

Even as he turned and made for the crevice, there was another violent shock. In the light of his headbeam, he saw the sides of the crevice coming together like snapping jaws.

Chapter Seven
GHOST BELLS

A sudden surge of water flung Troy towards the sealed crevice. As his headlamp swept over it, he found himself thinking that not even a spider crab could escape that way now.

Then the back surge sucked him away again, flinging him towards the darkness at the rear of the cavern. As he tumbled helplessly as a leaf caught in a gutter torrent, he got a glimpse of Marina in the light beam, spinning round and round, her hair streaming out behind her, her face pale and distorted with fear.

He tried to reach her, but she was snatched upwards out of the light as if by some giant invisible hand.

Then he found himself caught up and hurtled upwards, too, twisting in the grip of a powerful suction current.

Above him, in the light of his upturned lamp, he saw Marina being sucked into a round hole that suddenly gaped in the cavern roof. An instant later he was sucked in after her like a fly into a drain pipe.

There was a roaring in his ears, deafening him. He fumbled for the hydrophone control and switched it off, but even then he could still hear a muffled whooshing through the watertight insulated padding of the earpieces.

Up, up he went, whirling around, grazing the rock walls, hurtling up the shaft like a bullet through a gun barrel.

He lost all sense of time and was conscious only of that swirling water encasing him and the constant drumming in his ears.

After what seemed like eternity, the numbness that had gripped his mind eased and he became aware that he was whirling upwards less violently. He was able to make a conscious effort to look about him in the light of his headbeam, which had mercifully remained on in spite of the buffeting of the waters.

He was in a shaft about six feet across, smooth-walled and twisting slightly so that at times he was hurled from one wall to the other. He had to take care to protect his swim gear as well as himself from damage.

He looked up. Marina was just above him. Suddenly, she vanished. Fear gripped him for an instant and then he felt himself plucked almost at right angles to his course and sucked through a hole scarcely wide enough to take him and his air cylinders. For a brief moment, they snagged and he had an awful vision of himself being jammed in that hole like a cork in a bottle until his air supply gave out.

Then the pressure of the water behind him forced him out into calmer water. No longer did the current seem to have the strength to control him. He felt himself sinking slowly.

He looked down. His light beam showed Marina just below him, spiralling slowly downwards. To his relief, he saw she was swimming. He forced his own aching limbs into motion and followed her down. A few moments later, he saw she had stopped and then his flippered feet came to rest on a heap of loose rock and stone like scree at the foot of a mountain slope.

He looked up. They appeared to be at the bottom of a narrow rock basin whose walls stretched up into the darkness beyond the range of his light beam.

Remembering that borehole through which they had been sucked, he found himself thinking that it was just as if they had finished up in the bottom of the U bend of a sink drain pipe, except that they had been travelling the opposite way to the usual flow of water in plumbing. It was more as if the intense pressure created by the earth tremor had siphoned them here.

He realised they had been lucky. They might have been forced up a shaft too narrow to take them and squeezed to a pulp by the tremendous force of water below them, or they might have been shot out like lava from a volcano and smashed against the solid resistance of the comparatively still water above.

He switched on his hydrophone. To his relief, it was not damaged. The roaring still sounded in the headphones, but it was no longer deafening. But he saw that his chronometer depth-gauge was shattered. He must have struck it, without knowing, against the rock wall of the shaft.

He grinned at Marina. "Sure hope we haven't popped out of the frying pan into the fire? We'd better start looking for a way out."

She smiled and pointed upwards into the darkness.

"Guess you're right," he said. "If that water was still going upwards, I guess we can too."

They swam up cautiously. When they reached the hole in the rock wall through which they had come, the current plucked at them again, but it was much weaker now and merely assisted their passage upwards without impeding them.

The shaft went straight up for a hundred feet or so, and then the walls fanned out abruptly on all sides to form the rock bottom of what appeared to be a big subterranean chamber.

They swam around it, spiralling slowly upwards, examining the walls in the light of the headbeam. Nowhere did Troy see a fissure large enough to promise a way of escape.

Presently, Marina tugged at his arm and darted away obliquely towards the upper part of the chamber. He realised she had seen or sensed something beyond the range of his light, and he swam eagerly after her.

He found her at the entrance to another shaft leading out of the domed roof of the chamber. He shone his light into it. It slanted upwards at a steep angle and looked wide enough to take them comfortably.

Marina squeezed past him and swam up, and he followed, keeping her in the range of his light. The shaft ran fairly straight and widened gradually. Troy reckoned they had climbed several hundred feet before Marina stopped again. When he reached her she gestured to his headlamp and he switched it off.

Then, as his eyes adjusted themselves to the darkness, he saw beyond her a faintly light patch.

His heart leapt, for he was certain this could only mean they had found an outlet into the higher levels of the ocean where the sun's rays penetrated.

Then he remembered that topside it must still be night. Unless they were so near the surface that the moonlight—

Marina, who had been silhouetted against that lighter patch, as if peering before her, now turned and gripped his arm tightly, and he knew she was warning him. She had seen something.

What was it? Some monster of the deep lurking there, waiting to prey on them?

He pushed past her and peered cautiously out, his eyeshield just above the edge of the hole.

In the dim light, he saw that the shaft emerged from a rock wall onto an underwater shelf covered with grey-white silt and littered with small rocks. It stretched away into the gloom and somewhere out there he knew it must drop away into the sheer abyss of the great trench from which he and Marina had come.

A school of brightly coloured fish darted past, screening his view for a moment. When he could see again he spotted what Marina must already have seen—the source of that dim light.

Off to the right, almost on the edge of the range of his vision, was the illuminated cabin of an underwater craft.

It was Number Thirteen, the WASP patrol vessel that Conrad Hagen had hi-jacked way back in the North Pacific.

Marina joined him and they hung there, studying the vessel. There was no sign of movement about it, but that did not mean it was not occupied.

Was Atlanta still a prisoner in it, or had she been left elsewhere? There seemed to be only one way to find out.

He turned to Marina, and then, again, she gripped his arm with urgency. In the dim light, he could see her face as a pale blur. He saw her raise a hand and gesture towards her ear as if telling him to listen.

He did so but could hear nothing beyond the whisperings of the ocean creatures. Marina's ears were even more sensitive than his hydrophones at low volume and he gradually increased the power.

He now heard what she must have heard, and his heartbeat quickened. It was the slow, faint, yet unmistakable tolling of muffled bells.

"The bells of Sanito Cathedral!" he gasped, forgetting in his excitement that his voice might be picked up by the sensitive hydrophones in Number Thirteen.

Marina nodded eagerly.

So at least part of the legend Manco had told him was true! As for the rest, well, the presence of the stolen WASP vessel out there on the ledge seemed to indicate that Hagen, at any rate, believed in it.

Now that his chronometer was smashed, Troy could not tell for certain how much time had elapsed since they had left Stingray, but the hour he had set as the limit of his exploration must soon be up. If Phones heard nothing within another hour, he would come searching for them— and maybe run slap into trouble.

Troy dared not risk trying to contact Phones by hydrophone, for the message might be picked up by Hagen or his men, some of whom might still be out in the aquasprites.

He put his head close to Marina's.

"Get back to Stingray and tell Phones to stand by!" he whispered.

She looked at him mutely. He could not see the expression on her face, but he sensed she was asking him what he was going to do.

"I'm going to try to rescue Atlanta if she's in that vessel," he told her. "If I hit trouble I can't handle, I'll contact Phones."

Marina tried to protest– Atlanta was one of her closest friends among the surface dwellers– but he managed to convince her he stood a better chance alone. She squeezed his hand and then swam out of the shaft, hugging the bottom of the rock wall, and vanishing into the gloom towards the edge of the shelf.

Troy waited until she was well away, then swam out of the shaft.

That muffled tolling was still faintly audible. He wondered if it was only to be heard when an earth tremor had violently disturbed the water in which the cathedral sank many centuries before. It seemed as good a theory as any.

As he swam slowly through the murk just above the shelf towards the WASP vessel, he remembered something else that Manco had told him.

El Monstruo!

If the legendary monster that was said to guard the way to the lost treasure city of Sanito was as much a fact as the submerged cathedral bells...

He found himself looking around uneasily. After that horrific encounter with the giant sea anemone, he was in no mood to pooh-pooh stories of sea monsters.

Maybe that anemone or one of its breed was the monster? But brief reflection made him discard the idea. He felt it had been too far down for one thing, and any monster that gave rise to such a legend would be pretty mobile, he reckoned, like the giant squid.

The WASP vessel was plainly visible now, standing on its skids in the ooze, half-hidden as Stingray had been under a big rock overhang, its nose pointing towards the lip of the great trench.

He kept close to the rock wall so that if the scanners were working they would be less likely to pick him up against its background.

He was about fifty feet away when someone appeared at the control cabin window. It was Helga Hagen.

Troy flattened out against the silt near the wall. A startled crab scuttled away behind a small boulder. A colony of anemones hastily withdrew their tentacles into their mouths and a brittle star waltzed grotesquely away, waving its appendages like an underwater ballet dancer.

Helga was looking straight in his direction. He hugged the silt as close as he could without disturbing it. He did not think she had seen him, but if the silt was stirred into a cloud she might be curious.

He relaxed again as she moved away. He wondered if she were in the vessel alone, guarding Atlanta. That would make his task easier.

Slowly he went on, keeping just above the sea bottom. His flippers moved gently as they propelled him towards the rear of the vessel.

He saw movement in his peripheral vision. He flattened out again, clumsily, so that a cloud of grey silt rose like a puff of smoke into the water now illuminated by the cabin lights.

Helga was at the window again.

He cursed himself for panicking. If she saw that telltale cloud of silt…

Then he saw she wasn't looking in his direction, but away towards the trench edge where the deeps began.

Although he couldn't read her expression, he sensed that she was scared.

Something that looked like a huge elongated shadow swooped down into the light glow and struck the conning tower. Troy heard the impact over his hydrophones and saw the massive vessel rock on its skids. As he frantically turned the volume down, he saw that the stationary vessel had nearly turned over.

The shadow recoiled and vanished into the darkness again. Helga's scream of fear rang in his ears.

"Help! Father! Help! Come back!"

Troy peered up into the darkness beyond the range of the cabin lights. He sensed, rather than saw, something up there.

Something huge agitated the water violently.

And then that great shadowy thing swooped down again and struck the vessel with another crushing blow.

"Help!" Helga's panic-stricken voice echoed in the hydrophones.

He saw her fling herself away from the window, and the cabin lights went out, plunging the shelf on which he lay into darkness.

He heard another blow strike the vessel. Fierce angry creature noises sounded in his ears. Above him, the water was thrashed as if by some gigantic flail.

The shock waves thrust down at him, and he burrowed into the silt in near panic, expecting at any moment to be attacked by whatever was up there, venting its rage.

But all at once the sounds of fury faded and gradually the natural calm of the deep settled down again on the shelf.

Warily, Troy raised his head, conscious of the cold sweat streaming down inside his mask, a little ashamed now of his fear.

What had that been up there in the darkness?

El Monstruo?

A giant manta ray or a shark? A squid?

But the little he had seen of that vast shadow shape seemed to fit none of the monster denizens of the deep that he had encountered before.

It was obvious, though, that the lights of the WASP vessel must have attracted it and provoked its attack. Either it had thought it an enemy or something good to eat and Manco's grim words came back to him. "People who see it do not live to tell about it, senor."

He could well believe it.

He grinned brashly. But he had seen it and he was still alive. Maybe that was a good omen?

He swam on quickly towards the dark vessel. He could imagine Helga crouching in the cabin, petrified with fear, scared to switch on the lights again in case it induced the monster to resume its attack.

Now was his chance, if ever.

He saw the shape of the vessel looming up before him, faintly outlined by the luminescence of tiny creatures that had drifted against its hull, and groped his way towards the port aquasprite bay.

He was gambling on Hagen not knowing that the airlocks could be operated manually from outside so that in time of emergency they could be used as rescue hatches by knowledgeable members of the World Aquanaut Security Patrol.

A searchlight beam split through the darkness!

Troy dived down under the stern of the submarine and burrowed into the silt between the skids.

Along the shelf, the illumination was shining on the side of the vessel above him.

An aquasprite was flashing down towards it. Inside, he could see Hagen in the pilot's seat and José beside him.

Had they spotted him?

Then he heard Hagen's harsh impatient voice in his earphones. "Helga! What happened? Where are you?"

He heard the girl's gasped reply. "Thank heavens you've come, father! There—there's something terrible out there in the dark. It—it attacked the sub!"

"El Monstruo!" José gulped. Troy could see his face contorted with sudden fear. "It will eat us all!"

"Shut up, you darned jitterbug!" Hagen snarled. "We can handle it, whatever it is. Okay, Helga! Open the port airlock. We'll come aboard."

As the tiny craft disappeared into the parent vessel, Troy flashed out from beneath the latter and into the starboard bay.

The other aquasprite was there. He'd thought the other three thugs José recruited in Hatica a few hours earlier might have been out in it. As they weren't in the sub either, that could only mean they hadn't yet teamed up with Hagen.

"This thins the odds down a little," he muttered, pressing the button that manually operated the airlock hatch.

He was banking on Helga being so unfamiliar with the controls that she wouldn't notice that both bay pumps were working simultaneously.

As soon as the lock was free of water, Troy took off his flippers and mask and stepped into the compartment beyond. The lights were on. Hagen and José had to get out of the 'sprite before they could enter the compartment and these few moments of grace were all he needed to hide.

"I shouldn't have left her here alone," Hagen was growling as he came into the compartment, his bearded face flushed with annoyance. "She's scared of her own shadow."

"If senorita saw El Monstruo she saw no shadow, senor. In Hatica they say—"

"I don't care a bent nickel what those boneheads say," Hagen snarled. "We're not armed with pea-shooters. Guess it's just a giant ray or something."

The bulkhead door closed on them, and Troy slipped from his place of concealment behind a crate of stores and followed. He saw the two men going up the companionway to the control cabin. Moving with confidence now that he knew he had only to deal with the two men and Helga, Troy crept to the bottom of the stairway.

Up in the cabin, Helga was talking excitedly.

"But I tell you it wasn't like a ray, father. It—it wasn't like anything I've ever seen. It was a nightmare. It was so long I couldn't see the end of it. And its mouth—it looked big enough to swallow that little bug you were out in!"

"Caramba!" José gasped. "And she calls us to come back so it can swallow us!"

"Shut up, you fool!" Hagen snarled.

"Let's get away, father!" Helga went on urgently. "What with that horror and the earth tremors—"

"Take it easy, honey!" Hagen was shaking more calmly, trying to soothe her. "You had a fright, sure, but that's no reason for quitting just when we can see the end of the trail."

"End of the trail?" The girl's voice was less agitated now. "You mean—?"

79

"I figure we've found Sanito. Those bells! Did you hear 'em just now? Even this monster you saw. Guess it all fits the legend, Helga."

"Did you see the bells—the cathedral?"

"No. But there was a paved road and signs of ruins. Reckon if we'd gone on further we'd have found more ..." Silently Troy crept up the companionway, drawing his ray gun from its holster.

"But that treasure's not going to be easy to locate," Hagen went on. All three of them were standing by the control bank, their backs to Troy. "Your amigos, José, when do we pick them up?"

"Just before dawn, senor."

"It's after midnight now. We'll head that way and surface for a spell. Guess that'll make Helga feel happier."

"You're not going anyplace, Hagen!" Troy said quietly. "Except maybe back to jail!"

Hagen swung round with a startled gasp. His greenish eyes narrowed with hate when he recognised Troy. "Tempest!"

"La Tempestad!" José's face had gone a pale grey. "Santa Maria! How did he get here?"

Hagen got control of himself with a visible effort and smiled coldly. "You fool, Tempest! You'll never take me back to Marineville!"

"You wouldn't care to bet on that, mister?" Troy drawled. He looked at the girl, who was regarding him with a venom that contrasted strangely with the smiles she had bestowed on him at their last encounter. "There's a rope in that locker behind you, Miss Hagen. Get it and tie up your father and his sidekick."

Helga hesitated, looking at him defiantly, and her father sneered, "Call his bluff, honey. It's against his code to shoot a lady."

"But not to shoot rats!" Troy cut in bleakly. "Do as I say, Helga, or I'll give your father a blast in each leg. That should keep him out of action while I deal with you and José. It'll be painful for him."

"You devil!" Helga almost hissed the words at him, her eyes flashing.

She turned and opened the locker and took out the rope.

And then something struck the vessel. A terrific blow rocked the whole ship as Troy was flung back against the auxiliary instrument console. He got a glimpse of a hideous head with a gaping mouth filled with razor teeth outside the window.

Before he could recover his balance, the end of the rope snaked from Helga's hand and whipped about his face, half-blinding him with its stinging lash.

Staggering, Troy fell down the companionway. He hit the lower deck with a crash that drove the breath from his body and left him half-stunned. Before he could collect his senses, the two men hurled themselves down the stairway on top of him.

Chapter Eight
ESCAPE!

Dazed though he was, Troy fought back desperately, but José drove a vicious knee hard into his stomach and Hagen smashed a hammer fist to his jaw.

He went limp, the remaining strength draining out of him.

As if from down a long tunnel, he heard Helga screaming, and he was dimly conscious of the vessel shuddering violently.

"Switch off the lights!" he heard Hagen roar close to his ear, and then blackness swirled about him. He heard no more.

* * *

When Troy opened his eyes he was still in darkness. His head ached and there was a sore feeling in the pit of his stomach where José had struck him.

He tried to sit up but found he was bound hand and foot. He seemed to be lying on a carpeted floor and knew he was still somewhere in the submarine by the quivering and the low whine of the generator somewhere below him. It was evident that the vessel was now underway.

"Well, at least they haven't pushed me out of an airlock to pacify whatever it was out there," he muttered.

He shuddered when he recalled that hideous mouth. Helga hadn't been exaggerating when she'd told her father it looked big enough to swallow a 'sprite, he thought grimly.

He stiffened and strained his ears to listen above the whine of the motors. Something was working its way softly across the carpeted floor towards him.

"Who's there?" he challenged hoarsely.

"Shush! Not so loud, Troy! One of them may come back."

"Atlanta!"

She was beside him now, talking quietly. "They just tossed you into the sleeping quarters and went off in a hurry. It sounded as though something was trying to wreck the sub."

"Trying to make a meal of it, Atlanta," he acknowledged.

She began to cut his binds, and he told her about the monster he'd seen outside the vessel.

"Guess I've got to thank it for being here," he went on. "I had everything under control. Sewed up fine! Inside an hour I guess I could have reported mission accomplished to your father, then— wham!"

"You've got Stingray near?" she asked eagerly. "You found those buoys I released?"

"Sure! That was a smart trick, Atlanta. I bet Hagen's still wondering how I got on his trail so fast. You all right? He hasn't hurt you?"

"No. When he no longer wanted me to help navigate he kept me tied up on a bunk, but last time José didn't tie my hands too well. I'd just managed to work them free when they threw you in. They had a torch—that's how I saw it was you. What's happening?"

Briefly, he told her the situation. He was free now and rose to his feet, taking her by the arm in the dark and urging her towards the door.

"We've got to get away fast and contact Phones. When he brings up Stingray, we'll go after Hagen."

"Get out?" she gasped. "But they've taken your mask and air cylinders!"

"There'll be other gear in the equipment bay. We'll go out through the after-emergency hatch. Hurry! We've got to make it before they find out we're not here."

There were no locks on the door. It slid back smoothly and silently. Outside, the lower deck was in darkness. Only a faint glimmer of light filtered down the companionway from the instrument bank in the control cabin. Hagen was travelling without lights at around a hundred knots. Trying to shake off that monster, Troy told himself.

They crept into the equipment bay, and Troy switched on the light. There was no risk of being seen through the water-tight door and the bay had no windows. It was better than groping in the dark when every moment might be vital and yet there was so much to check before they could leave.

They put on the equipment, and Troy made sure each was fitted with chronometer-depth gauges and compasses, and that the first-aid satchel contained shark repellent.

He looked for guns too but could find none.

"Guess Hagen's collected all the small arms and put them where he can keep an eye on them," he whispered. "We'll have to make out with harpoon guns and knives."

She looked at him, her lovely face tense.

"You–you're thinking of that—that thing out there, Troy?"

He grinned tightly. "It's not the kind of thing you can forget. But it's either taking a chance out there or in here with this bunch of barracudas. Later Hagen will be picking up three more men, and then—"

"Sure, Troy! We wouldn't have the chance of a snowflake in an oven." Her chin stuck out bravely. She picked up a harpoon gun and checked it expertly. "Okay! Let's go!"

But Troy was well aware that the monster was not the only risk they had to face when leaving the submarine. To plunge straight out of the airlock into the slipstream, even at the comparatively slow speed that the vessel was travelling, would be as dangerous as leaping from a jet plane with a faulty parachute.

Troy took a hundred-fathom triple-braided line from the store locker, cut off a short length, and secured one end around his own waist. Then he tied on Atlanta with a few feet of link line between them.

When they entered the airlock, he twisted this link into a loop, through which he passed one end of the long line, and fastened it securely to a hook. He told Atlanta to grasp the rope with both hands some yards from the hook and only then did he operate the manual control that flooded the lock and opened the outer hatch.

When the hatch was fully open, Troy fixed a clamp to the edge so that it could not close completely on the line and sever it after they had gone. It would affect the vessel's navigation if the hatch didn't close and the lock remained full of water, but once they were clear he wasn't going to let that worry him. Hagen would discover their escape soon enough, anyway.

He flashed Atlanta a smile of encouragement. "Okay, honey," he said, gripping the line with both hands. "Let's bail out."

They slid out, Atlanta first, Troy close behind her. The sub's speed created a slight vacuum between its hull and the water. For a brief moment of time, they hung there in its comparative safety, and then the slipstream caught them, swinging them out along its V path, plucking at them like a live thing seeking to devour them. Troy thought his arms were going to be wrenched from their sockets. His breath seemed to be driven from his lungs by the terrific pressure, despite the protection of his pressurised mask.

In the darkness beyond his feet, he could make out the dim shape of Atlanta swinging a few yards from him. He was glad he had taken the precaution of putting her further towards the tail of the vessel, for he knew his body was screening her slightly against the battering force of the water through which they were being drawn.

And he knew that if her hands were wrenched from their hold on the line, the link rope between them would hold her, even though the strain on his own arms would then be terrific.

Slowly, he relaxed his grip on the line, allowing it to run inch by inch through his hands so that he slid back to Atlanta.

Facing her, holding the line just above her hands, he paused for a few moments, easing his muscles.

The roar of the water over the hydrophones was like continuous thunder. To speak was like trying to communicate in a hurricane. But he put his mask close to hers and shouted, and she knew what he wanted her to do.

Gradually, she eased her grip with one hand and reached back along the line, which was as taut as a rod.

He followed. Foot by foot, yard by yard, hand over hand they made their agonizing way towards the tail of the submarine.

Once Atlanta relaxed her hold too much and went hurtling backwards. The sudden shock broke Troy's grip and the rope seared through his hands like a red hot wire until he could get a firm hold again.

At last, they were beyond the vessel's tail, whirling about in the darkness of the ocean behind the vicious screw. They still had to take the last great gamble of releasing their hold on the line altogether, but the danger of being sucked round into the rotating eddy damper encasing the hydrojets was passed.

Three hundred feet behind the tail, Troy put his mask close to Atlanta's.

"Now!" he yelled.

They took a deep breath and let go simultaneously.

The water caught them, whipped them away, the free end of the line skimming through the loop in the thick rope connecting them.

Then they were clear of the rigid line, whirling about each other at the end of the link like two balls on a thrown bolas.

Now that they were no longer motivated by the pull of the submarine, the solid water rapidly exercised its braking action on them and presently they were floating in still water far behind the vessel.

The silence of the depths settled around them, broken only by the whispering sonics, bringing balm to their tortured ears. Darkness encircled them.

Troy took his torch from his belt and shone it on Atlanta's mask. She blinked back at him.

"Okay, honey?"

"Just about, I guess," she gasped. "In future, if I want fun I'll stick to the Big Dipper and the Flying Chairs—or maybe I'll go for a trip with Venus in Fireball."

He chuckled. Atlanta was a chip off the old block for sure.

A shoal of angelfish swam past and Troy told himself they could not be very deep. He switched on the depth gauge and saw it registered thirty fathoms.

"My hunch is we're pretty close inshore," he said. "Let's go topside and take a look around."

They swam up and trod water. The ocean was calm and the moon, well down in the western sky, cast a long lane of yellow light towards them. But dawn was still three hours away.

Troy estimated they were some three miles offshore. The lights of a village glowed like fireflies, and beyond them, the dark majestic bulk of the Andes climbed against the starry cobalt of the heavens.

"Hagen's keeping a rendezvous with José's cut-throat amigos about three hours from now," Troy said. "That gives us plenty of time to make contact with Phones and maybe prepare a little reception for those sharks when they come back to look for Sanito."

"You think they will be back?" she asked doubtfully. "Won't it scare them off when they find we've escaped? They'll know Stingray will be hunting for them."

"Hagen'll be back. He's pretty sure there's a fortune waiting down there, and he won't give up without a fight. He's still got a pretty powerful weapon in Number Thirteen, and if he gets half a chance to blow Stingray out of the water, he'll do it for the sheer kick of it."

"Just to get his revenge on Dad you mean!"

"Comes to the same thing," he said with a tight grin. "But I'm not getting tangled in a shooting match, not unless there's absolutely no choice. I aim to take Number Thirteen back in one piece, and that goes for Hagen too. I'm not worried about his sidekicks."

"José seems a mighty jittery guy. Could be he and his amigos won't come, anyway, whatever Hagen does."

"They'll come, for the same reason as Hagen. From what I heard in that cantina, it's my hunch they're planning to doublecross him."

Atlanta laughed shortly. "From one or two things I overheard between Hagen and his daughter, I guess they're planning to do the same to José."

"Swell bunch of sea scorpions! Let's go!"

Troy dived down towards the sea bed and then swam south by west towards the great trench running parallel with the coast.

He'd roughly calculated their position– based on the speed of Number Thirteen and the time it had taken him and Atlanta to escape– as twenty-five miles north of the shelf where he'd boarded the submarine. So, if Phones had kept Stingray in her original position on that ledge down in the trench, she was some twenty miles south of them now.

"We're just about the limit of our hydrophone range," he told Atlanta. "But we'll keep calling him as we swim back. The sooner he picks us up the better."

"You're telling me," she said. "If we can't contact him, it's going to take us all of five or six hours to get back." When they reached the trench they turned due south above it, so there was as much clear water as possible between them and Stingray's position to aid communication.

Twice at three-minute intervals, Troy sent out his call sign without any response, but at the third call Phones came through immediately.

Troy gave him their approximate position and a few minutes later they saw the welcome lights of Stingray's cabin glowing through the darkness.

Phones already had coffee and sandwiches waiting for them, while Marina was tending to her injuries from the anemone. As they navigated Stingray back along the trench, the four friends told their stories.

"Seems everybody around here gets fun but me," Phones growled. "Guess I'm just the office boy."

"Quit beefing, pal," Troy said seriously. "If my hunch is right you'll have all the fun you can take a few hours from now. Contact base. Guess we ought to put the commander's mind at rest about Atlanta."

When the WASP chief came through, Phones handed the microphone over to Atlanta and let her tell him the great news herself.

"I'm not going to forget this in a hurry, Troy," Shore said presently, his gruff voice barely concealing his emotion. "If anything had happened to her... What are you aiming to do now?"

"Complete my mission, sir. You told me to go get Hagen—and get him good."

"Yeah. Well, that still stands. You want any help?"

"Even if I did, I reckon you couldn't get it to me in time, sir. Guess Stingray can handle it. I'm bringing Hagen and Number Thirteen back if I can."

"Great! But no black marks if you don't, captain, so long as you nail the shark. What about Atlanta? Are you putting her ashore someplace?"

Troy glanced at Atlanta, who was regarding him with mock ferocity. He grinned.

"If you make that an order, sir, I guess we'll have a mutiny on our hands."

"I can imagine!" the commander chuckled. "Well, if you can do with an extra hand I'll second her as assistant navigator. I guess she's earned it, but for Pete's sake see she doesn't get into more trouble."

"Okay, sir!"

As Phones switched off, he said, "Dollars to doughnuts Hagen picked that up, Troy."

"It wouldn't tell him anything he didn't know or couldn't work out for himself."

"Maybe not. Do we go get him right away, when he surfaces to pick up those roughneck amigos of José's?"

"Guess that's just what he'll be expecting us to do, Phones, so it wouldn't be a smart move, even if we knew just where he's picking 'em up. We'll call the tune. When he comes back we'll be waiting for him." Troy glanced at the chronometer. "Reckon we've got just about three hours to prepare a surprise for him. Reconnaissance rate one. We'll take a look around that shelf where he parked Number Thirteen. Maybe it'll give us ideas."

Troy took Stingray down a thousand feet into the trench, keeping well away from the rock walls, so that the scanners would immediately pick up anything that approached.

Phones grinned at him. "Playing it safe, pal? El Monstruo got you scared?"

Troy smiled grimly. "Brother, you'd be scared if you'd had him breathing down your neck like I did."

He switched off the cabin lights as they neared the shelf, then brought Stingray up slowly, scanners probing. Nothing of any great size registered. They waited, like a moray eel, for their prey to return to the deep darkness of the ocean trench.

* * *

Troy wasn't kidding when he'd told Phones the monster scared him. Nobody in his right mind could pretend he wasn't scared of a creature like that. But inside the protection of Stingray's prestressed hull, his fear was not a personal one. He didn't doubt that the super sub could survive any attack the creature made on it, and a sting missile down its cavernous throat would soon settle the issue.

Yet he saw no sense in deliberately courting attack. His main objective now was to get Hagen and recapture Number Thirteen. A fin or a hydroplane damaged in a battle with the monster would seriously handicap him when the showdown with Hagen came.

As Stingray rose above the level of the shelf, they all peered out anxiously, but nothing hurtled out of the blackness of the water to attack them as it had attacked Number Thirteen.

"Maybe he's having his breakfast," Phones said. His jocular tone could not disguise the relief in his voice.

Troy set Stingray gently down on the spot under the protecting overhang of rock where Hagen had parked Number Thirteen earlier.

"I'll take out a 'sprite and reconnoitre this shelf," Troy said as the whine of the motors died away. "Want to come, Phones?"

"Sure."

Troy grinned mischievously. "Helga said that thing had a mouth big enough to swallow a 'sprite whole."

"Yeah? Well, if he wants indigestion that's his lookout, pal!" Phones retorted. "This is one trip I'm not missing."

Troy decided to take swim gear, just as a precaution.

"You girls sit tight," he said. "If anything scares you, call us and we'll be right back."

Atlanta's hazel eyes flashed. "And if anything scares you!"

"We'll be right back, anyway," Phones chuckled.

The two WASPs entered the tiny craft and a few moments later were seaborne. As they sped away from Stingray, Troy saw the faces of his friends peering out from the darkened cabin.

They were tough as girls came, but he wondered if he was doing right in leaving them alone. Maybe it would be better to stick together?

Then he pushed his doubts from his mind. They were safe enough inside the super sub and could handle Stingray between them almost as well as he and Phones.

"Just before Helga called Hagen back because she was scared of that monster, Hagen had seen something along here," he told Phones.

"Like what?"

"A paved road and ruins. He was certain it was part of Sanito."

Phones glanced at him curiously. "You're not aiming to go treasure-hunting to pass the time, Troy?"

"Nope, I was just thinking that Hagen's going to find treasure in Sanito or bust. If we could find it first…"

"We could do the busting?"

Troy grinned. "Something like that."

* * *

On the Isle of Lemoy, thousands of miles to the north, surface agent X-20 was genuflecting before his master's image on the big video screen that had risen from the floor of his drab living room.

"News, O Mighty Titan! Commander Shore has just received a report from Tempest. He has rescued Shore's daughter from the Terrainean pirate, Conrad Hagen."

"Bah!" Titan's cruel face suffused with rage. "A thousand curses on Tempest! Did I not warn you this would happen, shrimp spawn?"

"Yes, O Mighty One! Your wisdom is great."

"As I prophesied, Tempest has destroyed this fool Hagen, of course?"

"No, master! Tempest rescued her by cunning. Hagen is still free. Tempest plans to capture him and bring him back to Marineville to stand trial."

"So?" Titan sneered. "Sometimes I wonder if Captain Tempest is not something of a fool. He tries to be too clever. So this Hagen is still free?"

"Yes, O Mighty King!"

Titan frowned thoughtfully. "Where is Hagen?"

"Somewhere off the Terrainean town of Hatica, near the southern border of the surface nation known as Peru, master."

"Good!"

Titan vanished from the screen.

"Alas," sighed X-20. "He didn't even say goodbye!"

* * *

In his throne room in Titanica, Titan addressed an aquaphibian who had been waiting at the foot of the steps leading to his throne.

"Contact the commander of the quartz mines in Region Seven. Tell him to place a squadron of mechanical fish at my disposal immediately."

"But, O Mighty One, already Stingray has destroyed one squadron—"

"Imbecile! Do you think your ruler so senile that I have to be reminded of the accursed fact? Do as I bid, and order the commander to report to me by videophone instantly."

"It shall be done, Mighty Titan!" quavered the aquaphibian, bowing itself out.

Chapter Nine
TERROR IN THE DARK

W hile Phones kept a wary eye open for the monstrous creature that had attacked Number Thirteen, Troy raked the shelf and the face of the rock slope beyond with the aquasprite's searchlight beam.

The shelf was about four hundred yards across at its widest and over two miles long, covered inches thick with silt that had drifted down from the continental slope high above it.

The rock face continued down into the abyss of the trench itself and was serrated with fissures, most of them narrow and partly silted up. Those that looked wide enough to take the 'sprite soon narrowed, making further exploration of them impossible.

"You reckon Hagen could have imagined seeing that paved road, Troy?" Phones asked at length.

"Not Hagen! Besides, he said he heard the bells too."

Troy looked up thoughtfully to where the rock wall vanished into the darkness. "When I first saw him coming back to Number Thirteen after Helga screamed for help, he was coming down at an angle. Let's take a look higher up, Phones."

They rose three hundred feet and cruised back along the rock slope, probing the beam into every fissure and hollow.

Suddenly, Phones spoke, "That one looks big enough to take a 'sprite, Troy."

He was pointing at a fissure, slit-narrow at the base, but widening into a V-shaped cleft rising beyond the ledge towards which they were climbing.

"Sure does," Troy said, taking the 'sprite above the ledge and probing the cleft with the searchlight. It went beyond the limits of the beam. "Try another scanner sounding, Phones."

Anxiously, they watched the graph on the small instrument panel before them.

"Five hundred-plus feet," Phones announced at last. "And the echoes could be from a bend and not a block, I guess."

"The deepest we've found yet, anyway. We'll take a look inside."

Slowly, they cruised into the cleft, the light beam carving a cone through the blackness ahead of them. A funnel whose lateral curves were flattened by the light splashing on the solid rock of the fissure walls.

A flat, white, worm-like fish darted into the light with a wriggling motion and then twisted away into the darkness again. Here and there the light touched on glistening clusters of molluscs clinging to the walls. A hundred and twenty feet inside, the cleft acquired a rough roof and became a tunnel just wide enough to take the little craft and they had to keep the scanners working constantly to avoid scraping the sides and possibly damaging the vanes.

At five hundred feet they found that Phones' hunch had been right. The tunnel turned at a sharp angle. Excitement stirred them now as they went on cautiously into the heart of the rock.

Presently, the roof rose again and the tunnel became a tortuous defile where every bend was a minor hazard to be negotiated.

Phones suddenly gasped, "Say, listen, Troy!"

He switched on the hydrophone speaker and Troy's pulses raced when he heard the slow muffled tolling of a bell.

"This is it, Phones! This is what Hagen must have heard. Marina and I heard it because the shock waves from that tremor must have carried the sound outside."

"Maybe that paved road Hagen saw can't be far away."

Three hundred feet further on the defile gradually widened and they emerged into a subterranean cavern whose bottom was thick with silt. As the light beam swept around it, Phones cried out.

"There it is, Troy!"

Troy took the craft in the direction of his pointing finger and his heart leapt when he saw what appeared to be the shattered remnants of a road paved with large slabs of hewn stone. It was canted at a steep angle that had not held the silt. The lower end disappeared below the sludge, the upper being abruptly cut off by the rock wall of the cavern. It seemed as if the edge of a rock fault, triggered by that calamity in the long distant past, had come down on the road like a guillotine blade.

Troy swept the beam around the cavern. A few yards from one side of the broken road was a jumble of masonry blocks, fashioned by old tools.

"The ruins of some building that had once stood near the road," he murmured.

He told himself that there might have been other buildings here where disaster overwhelmed Sanito, but if they had been constructed of brick or adobe or timber, they would have disintegrated into the sediment long ago.

"Hagen said he couldn't go any further," Troy said. "But he might have missed something. The odds are the earthquake that destroyed Sanito pushed this section a long way from the rest of the——"

"Troy!" There was a strained note in Phones' voice. "Something's moving in behind us!"

Even as he spoke, Troy felt the tiny craft rock as if a pressure wave had pushed against it.

He swung the 'sprite round, almost in its own length, and the sweeping light beam flashed across a huge dark shape that was surging through the water from the depths of the cavern.

A vast eye, as big as a dinner plate, glinted briefly in the light.

Ice needles pricked along Troy's spine. Instinctively, he flicked off the searchlight, plunging the cavern into darkness and flung the 'sprite upwards into a vertical climb.

It bucked wildly in the wash of something colossal that plunged headlong beneath it and struck the wall of the cavern with a dull thud that could be plainly heard over the loudspeaker which Phones had left switched on after hearing the bells.

"Troy!" yelled Phones, in near panic. "We're going to smash against the roof!"

Like lightning Troy reacted, bringing the vessel round in a sharp loop. As it dived steeply, its nose struck something with a crash that almost flung him from his seat. It was something that wasn't hard enough to be rock and yielded slightly under the impact.

As the 'sprite rebounded, wallowing out of control for an instant, something struck it again, hurling it through the dark water like a ball from a bat.

Troy felt it scrape the wall before he brought it under control and sent it up towards the roof again.

"We've got to get out of here, Troy!" Phones gulped.

"I'm on your side, brother," Troy gritted between set teeth. "But just where is the way out?"

"I can't use the scanners while we're being tossed about like this," Phones assessed. "We've got to have light, Troy."

"If it's what I think it is, it's the light that attracts it."

"Then use a contact flare, for Pete's sake!"

Phones' voice rose in a crescendo of alarm as another violent blow struck the vessel, flinging it across the cavern, while angry creature noises sounded over the speaker.

Troy fumbled for the flare gun control and triggered it. A tiny missile hissed from its tube and sped upwards through the darkness. An instant later it struck the roof and exploded in a brilliant blue-white flare that lit up the cavern like an arc lamp.

For a moment the flare blinded Troy.

And then he saw it!

The creature must have been almost eighty feet long and more than ten feet thick, with huge jaws bristling with razor teeth, wicked glaring eyes, and long ribbon fins stretching down its spine and belly to its flattened tail.

"What in the name of Neptune is it?" Phones gasped.

In the numbness of Troy's stunned mind, a memory cell clicked.

"It looks like a monster conger eel, Phones," he said hoarsely.

His skin crawled as the monster thrashed wildly. Ordinary congers a mere six or eight feet long could inflict ghastly damage. Once they got a grip on a man's limb they would not let go, and even after they'd been killed their powerful jaws would have to be prised apart to release their victim.

The flare was drifting slowly through the black water. The eel hurtled itself at it, great jaws agape, and the cavern was plunged into darkness again as the flare vanished down the vast gullet.

Troy hesitated to attribute intelligence to the monster, but he sensed it had seen the 'sprite and in the darkness, it was the master of the situation. One snap of those jaws would crush the 'sprite like an egg!

He sent the little craft diving down towards the jumble of masonry that had once been a splendid building in Sanito, switching on the searchlight because speed at that moment was more vital than concealment.

The creature was slow in turning its sinuous length in the confines of the cavern and Troy had the 'sprite among the ruins before the great torpedo shape came swooping down like a jet dive bomber.

It crashed against the massive blocks of stone. They shuddered under the shock. Again and again, it charged the ruins. Above the furious noises, Troy could hear teeth slashing at the solid stone as if trying to tear it apart to get at the 'sprite.

Only when he switched off the lights did it cease its attacks. As it swam away, its wash coursed between the stones, rocking the 'sprite, and then the dark water became calm again.

Still, Troy hesitated to emerge from the protection of the ruins. What if it was being canny, lying dormant out there on the bottom of the cavern, waiting for them to venture out?

He realised that cold sweat was streaming down him. He'd been in some tight spots since joining the WASPs, but seldom one as terrifying as this.

Phones was the first one to break the silence.

"I sure hope that flare gives him a stomachache," he growled.

They burst out laughing, glad to relieve the tension.

"I'll try another flare and see if it really has beat it," Troy said.

He aimed the flare at the roof. It exploded and the cavern was flooded with light again.

"If it's still around, I'll try a missile on it this time," Troy said as they peered out anxiously.

But there was no sign of the monster, to Troy's relief. He had a feeling that the small missiles the 'sprites carried would do no more than sting the creature into greater fury unless he could be lucky enough to plant one in a vital spot. But where was the vital spot in a monster like that?

For the first time, something curious occurred to Troy.

"How the blazes did it get in here, Phones? It's too big to have come the way we did."

"You're dead right, Troy. That means there must be another way into the cavern."

"Unless there are two of those nightmares—one inside and one outside. But that seems to be stretching coincidence too far."

As the flare drifted slowly down, they emerged from the shelter of the ruins, looking about them for some sign of an opening big enough to pass the monstrous eel, but they could see none. The fissure through which they had come was the biggest aperture they could find.

"But it sure couldn't vanish——"

"Into thin water, you mean?" Phones laughed mirthlessly.

"Yeah. It had to go somewhere, Phones, and where it went we could go. It could lead to the rest of the submerged city."

"Don't push our luck too far, Troy," Phones said. "If we were in Stingray, I'd be all for it but in this little nutshell——"

"Guess you're right, Phones," Troy said reluctantly as the flare faded. "We'd need a sting missile to take care of that baby." He switched on the searchlight and sent the little vessel gliding across the cavern to the fissure through which it had brought them. "Let's get back and report to the girls."

As the 'sprite sped into the fissure, Phones chuckled.

"What's so funny?" Troy asked.

"I was thinking there's no need for us to cook up a little surprise for Hagen and his bunch. That critter back there will give them the time of their——Hello!"

Phones jerked up suddenly, looking at the instrument bank.

"What's wrong, Phones?"

"The seismograph's registering an earth tremor. Pretty big."

The words were scarcely out of Phones' mouth before Troy felt the pressure wave strike the little craft, urging it forward along the defile.

His throat went tight. He remembered what had happened down there in that cavern in the great trench where he had rescued Marina from the monster sea anemone and how the rock walls of the passage had snapped together like jaws. If anything like that happened now...

He increased the 'sprite's speed as much as he dared. The tremor persisted, causing the seismograph needle to flicker crazily.

They reached the place where the fissure became a tunnel and sped into it. Another few hundred feet and they would be in the safety of deep water.

Abruptly, he cut the motor and fired the emergency retro-hydrojets, bringing the 'sprite to a halt just inside the tunnel exit.

Beyond it, the water was murky, like a thick fog, which the searchlight beam could not penetrate more than a few feet.

"The scanner's pinging like crazy!" Phones exclaimed. "What's going on out there?"

"That's mud and debris falling, almost solid matter, I guess. We'd never get through, Phones."

"You mean it's an underwater avalanche?"

"Yes. A turbidity current, bringing down thousands of tons of stuff from the continental slope. That tremor must have triggered it off."

Troy had read about turbidity currents, but he'd never seen one in action before. Neither had many people. Only a few years back even expert scientists had scoffed at the theory put forward by some oceanographers that these deepwater currents existed, charging down the steep continental slope at over fifty miles an hour, carrying all before them, gouging canyons and altering seascapes.

Twenty minutes later the silt was blocking off the tunnel like a solid wall.

* * *

Out on the shelf at the foot of the rock face, Atlanta felt the earth tremor rock Stingray. It scared her for a moment, but she'd experienced such shocks before and would have thought little more of this one had Marina not caught her arm and pointed agitatedly at the darkness above them.

"What's wrong, Marina?" she asked. "What can you see?"

For an answer, the other girl sprang to the pilot's seat and triggered the powerful motors into life, sending Stingray sliding off the shelf and hurtling in a wide arc out over the great deep of the trench.

Atlanta slid into Phones' seat beside Marina, knowing that her friend would not have behaved like this unless there was some urgent reason. She watched, with a sense of foreboding, as Marina brought the super sub round to face the shelf they had just left, then a cry of protest burst from her when Marina switched on the powerful searchlight beams.

"Marina! The monster!"

She broke off as Marina gestured urgently towards the rock face, and her heart contracted in horror at what she saw.

The slope was no longer visible in the light of the beam. It had completely vanished behind a grey-white curtain of muddy water. A torrent had rushed down from the darkness to the shelf where a few minutes ago Stingray had been resting. There it billowed out like smoke and charged across the shelf to plunge into the depths twenty thousand feet below.

Down and down it rushed. There seemed no end to it. All Atlanta could see was a vast wall of grey-white stretching out of sight in both directions.

"You saved us, Marina! But—Troy! Phones!" she gasped. "They—they must have been up there somewhere. We've got to look for them. Maybe they got clear in time, but the 'sprite could be damaged."

Marina flashed her a compassionate smile and took Stingray closer. The agitated water thrust around the ship and it took all the power of its motors to keep it on an even keel. For miles in either direction and far into the depths they searched, probing the murk with the searchlights, for the scanners were useless with so much fast-falling debris around.

In their anxiety for their lost friends, all thought of danger from the monster creature of the deep was banished from their minds.

And all the time they searched that tremendous river of mud cascaded into the abyss and the hydrophones rumbled as if with continuous thunder. For almost half an hour the fall continued, and then it ceased as abruptly as it had begun. The last murmur of thunder died away and the silence of the ocean depths descended once more on the cruising Stingray.

Atlanta gestured wearily to Marina and the girl from the sea steered Stingray close to the rock face in the direction the Auburn-haired lieutenant had pointed. The shelf on which the vessel had been grounded was no longer visible, buried hundreds of feet deep under a vast slope of silt, smooth and grey-white. The underwater landscape was dotted here and there by boulders that had been caught up in the torrent.

Atlanta switched on the hydrophone transmitter.

"Stingray calling Troy! Stingray calling Troy! Where are you?"

Again she sent out the urgent call as they cruised along the slope. But there was no reply. She hung up for fear of alerting Hagen to their distress.

Atlanta looked down in despair at that huge wall of silt piled up above the shelf. Did their friends lie crushed in their tiny craft somewhere under those tons and tons of mud?

Marina gripped her arm and smiled at her as if she had read her thoughts and was seeking to give her encouragement.

She pointed to the slope higher up, where bare rock glistened in the light beam.

"You mean they may have been able to take cover before the fall started?" Atlanta asked eagerly. "I hope you are right, Marina! But they may be trapped. We'll search every fissure."

They cruised above the silt line, probing every nook and cranny with scanners and searchlight, hosing away the silt wherever they thought they might find a lead to the missing aquasprite.

Suddenly, Marina grabbed her friend and pointed to her ears. Atlanta switched on the hydrophone speaker, and Marina's face lit up when she heard that solemn muffled tolling.

Atlanta cried, "The bells! I can hear the bells! Is that what you heard when you were with Troy?"

Marina nodded eagerly.

"If Troy also heard them, he would have tried to locate the source. I'm going to play a hunch that he's in there somewhere looking for them, maybe unable to get out again. But that sound must be coming to us along a water channel, so there must be a way in. We've got to locate it, Marina."

Patiently, Atlanta manipulated the hydrophone controls, while Marina took Stingray slowly backwards and forwards across the slope. Occasionally, bursts of sonics drowned the tolling of the bells altogether. Sometimes the sound faded abruptly as if being screened.

But, at last, Atlanta pointed to a large fissure half-hidden by silt.

"I'm certain it's coming from there," she exclaimed. "It looks big enough to fit Stingray, but if it narrows too much we can always take to the other aquasprite." She looked at Marina. "Are you game to try?"

The girl from the sea gave her hearty agreement.

* * *

A mile off the Peruvian coast Conrad Hagen stood in the conning tower of Number Thirteen, looking towards the few scattered lights that marked the sleeping town of Hatica.

"Still an hour to go before we pick up your amigos," he said to José. "Pity we didn't make it earlier. The sooner we get started the better."

"Maybe now they think it is too soon, senor."

Hagen looked at his dark figure sharply. "What d'you mean?"

José shrugged. "They will not be happy when they know that Stingray is in these waters."

"Stingray would have been no threat if Tempest hadn't got away, fool!" Hagen snarled. "If you'd made sure that girl was tied up properly–"

"Don't squabble over spilt milk, father!" Helga cut in irritably. "Maybe José's right. This thing doesn't look so good with Tempest breathing down our necks. Maybe we ought to quit while we can."

"I'm not quitting," Hagen said stubbornly. "And neither are you, honey. That stuff's down there somewhere and we're going to get it, even if it means blowing Stingray and Tempest to high heaven. But José can quit if he wants it that way," he went on viciously. "He can quit right now, and swim ashore."

"Senor!" The South American's voice quivered with fear. "I not say I quit. It's just that my amigos——"

"Shut up!" Helga snapped. "Something's coming. A boat, I think."

"A boat?" Hagen snarled. "It's coming up from below. It's a sub!"

"Stingray!" José gasped. "We are finished!"

A searchlight blazed on them, pinning the startled trio in the conning tower, then a cold gurgling voice said, "Do not move, Terraineans, or we shall destroy you."

Hagen looked at the dim fish-like shape that floated on the water behind the light, which appeared to come from one of the eyes of the strange craft.

"Who are you?" he demanded raspingly. "What the blazes d'you want with us?"

"My master, King Titan, wants to talk to you."

"Titan!" José gasped. "Diablo! We jump from the frying pan into the fire!"

Chapter Ten
TITAN STRIKES A BARGAIN

Conrad Hagen looked uneasily through his face mask at the four aquaphibians, armed with ray guns, who were ushering them through a rock passage far below the surface of the ocean.

Hagen did not scare easily, but there was something about those hideous half-human beings that sent cold shivers down his spine.

"Titan is a monster," José quavered in his earphones. "He will put us to the death of a thousand stings or have us pulled apart by lobsters."

"Shut up!" Hagen snarled at him. "It's bad enough to look at these horrors without having you—"

He broke off, looking about him in amazement, as they emerged into a huge cavern lit by globes of phosphorescence. Scores of aquaphibians and other primitive underwater creatures were working on ledges on its steep walls, laboriously slicing away slabs of pure quartz and loading them into huge clam shells powered by hydro-jets, which conveyed them across the cavern to where other aquaphibians loaded them into the hold of a big fish-shaped freighter craft.

The Hagens and José were taken across the submarine quarry and into a small cave where an aquaphibian in a red cloak sat at a rock desk, scratching entries on thin sheets of mother of pearl with a diamond-tipped coral stylo.

The escort halted and bowed slightly.

"Commander!" one of them said in its strange, gargling voice. "We have brought the Terraineans."

107

The aquaphibian in the red cloak surveyed Hagen and his companions with his big sinister fish eyes as if they were something that had been dragged out of the ocean ooze.

"Good!"

Hagen bridled. "Listen, crab face!"

"Silence, Terrainean fool! You were not brought here to insult me, but to be granted audience with his majesty, King Titan."

The commander got to his feet and went to one of the walls of the cave and operated a control. A big video screen lit up and the image of Titan appeared on it. The commander bowed low.

"Well?" Titan demanded. "Have you carried out my instructions?"

"Yes, O Mighty Titan. The Terraineans are here. They await your orders."

"Orders? Say, look here," Hagen objected, "I'm not taking orders from that—"

"Silence!" Titan thundered. "Bring the loud-mouthed imbecile before me!"

Hagen was thrust forward at the point of a gun.

Titan sneered contemptuously at him.

"So this is the Terrainean pirate who makes mighty plans but has not the brains to carry them out properly?"

"Say, listen, mister—"

"Silence! You kidnapped the daughter of the accursed Shore, yet allowed Tempest to snatch her from you single-handed. You had Tempest at your mercy, yet did not destroy him. That brands you as a fool! But even fools have their uses. I shall strike a bargain with you, Terrainean!"

"Yeah? What if I refuse to bargain—?"

"Then you are an even bigger fool than I thought!" Titan smiled coldly. "I always have need of slaves in my mines. The mortality rate is unavoidably high. And if you refuse to work, there is the lobster pit, where the commander keeps our crustacean friends with very little food. Your daughter would make a tasty morsel."

Helga uttered a strangled cry, and Hagen's flesh crawled.

"Okay," he growled. "What d'you want?"

"You are seeking the submerged city of Sanito. You believe treasure is buried there in the King's warehouse. You are right. There is much silver bullion. I shall let you have it."

"Oh, you will, huh?" snorted Hagen. "That's mighty kind of you, Mister Titan, but I guess it ain't yours to—"

"Idiot! I lay claim to all the treasures of the deep. Any Terrainean who tries to steal them incurs my displeasure. But the treasure of Sanito is silver, for which I have little use. Unlike gold and pearls and other precious stones, it corrodes and tarnishes in the sea. I shall allow you to take it and help you to defeat Troy Tempest."

Hagen's eyes narrowed suspiciously. "You said a bargain. What d'you get out of this?"

Titan's face twisted in a cruel smile. "I want Tempest. His crew and Commander Shore's daughter—alive. You can help me. Tempest, being a fool, if a dangerous one, is determined to capture you alive if possible and take the vessel you stole back to Marineville. That gives us a great advantage over him, for he will hesitate to use lethal weapons against you."

"So you're using us as bait, huh?"

Titan shrugged, his face a cynical mask. "You have a choice, Terrainean. If you do not like my terms…"

"Okay!" Hagen growled. "You win!"

"Perhaps you are not quite such a fool as you seem. As the first fruits of our partnership, my aquaphibians will show you an easy way to Sanito. But first, you have others of your expedition to collect, I believe?"

"You know a devil of a lot, Mister Titan!"

"I know everything that affects my well-being, Terrainean."

* * *

Troy Tempest looked grimly at the wall of silt that blocked the exit of the tunnel. It gave a foot or so before the probing nose of the aquasprite and then closed around it like a mould.

"We'll never get through, Phones," he said. "There must be hundreds of tons above us. Stingray might have made it with a suction pump, but I guess we'll have to go back to that cavern and find out how that overgrown eel got out."

"Yeah. If it was outside in the deep a while back, scaring the daylights out of Helga Hagen, then there must be some way through. We've just got to find it, Troy, before Hagen gets back and maybe finds Stingray."

There was no room in the tunnel to turn. Slowly, Troy reversed the little craft, easing it past the point where the tunnel angled sharply. He was a little worried that the silt might have fallen into the defile which led into the cavern, but to his relief it was clear and he was able to turn the 'sprite.

Troy stopped just inside the entrance to the cave and played the searchlight beam about it. It could not probe to the deepest recesses of the cavern, but he knew that if the monster conger was there it would attack the light, and they were safe from its fury inside the defile.

No huge shape hurtled out of the darkness at them and Troy sent the 'sprite slowly into the cavern.

"Odd the way it attacks light," Phones mused. "It gobbled up that flare as though it was something good to eat."

"Maybe that's the truth of it," Troy said. "Down in the depths most fish are illuminated so that if it sees a light, instinct prompts it to try to swallow it."

"What they call a light lunch, huh?" Phones grinned.

"Any more weak cracks like that and you can get out and walk," Troy growled.

They had circled the cavern four times in a spiralling course, probing the roof and walls with all the tools at their disposal when Phones broke the silence with an exclamation.

"Those bells! I'm picking 'em up on the hydrophones again, Troy. I'll see if I can trace the source."

Water is an amazing conductor of sound, Troy knew, and the deeper the water the greater the sound velocity, owing to the greater pressure. A volcanic rumble could be picked up thousands of miles away. But down there in those confined spaces, where the energy of the sound waves would be rapidly absorbed by rock walls, the source was not always easy to locate.

This time, though, Phones had little difficulty in pinpointing the sound source as a shallow cave-opening some two feet high at silt level, not far from the ruins of the paved road.

"Guess we've been looking too high," Troy said, focussing the light beam in the opening.

"But that overgrown eel couldn't have gotten through there," Phones objected.

"I guess an eel could burrow, and if that cave entrance is silted up—"

"You mean there could be a tunnel down there?"

"We'll take a look. We can't lose anything," Troy said, pushing the nose of the little vessel slowly into the silt below the low arch.

"Not unless we meet that feller coming back," Phones mused.

"You think of the darndest things, pal! You're a proper Jonah!"

"Yeah!" Phones grinned flatly. "That's what worries me. Finishing up playing Jonah to that whale of a conger."

They lapsed into silence as they probed deeper into the silt. The cave opening was just high enough to permit Troy to keep the transparent upper casing of the aquasprite above the silt, but the searchlight couldn't be used because it was buried, so they had to feel their way forward in the limited range of the cabin lights.

After they had gone twenty yards or so, however, the roof of the cavern began to rise sharply and presently they emerged from the ooze again. The cave, some twenty feet wide at this point, stretched away before them into the darkness, narrowing gradually.

"Sure seems your bet came up, Troy," Phones muttered. "Looks like a tunnel leading someplace."

"Yeah."

Troy's mouth was a little dry. Negotiating an unknown tunnel in the dark, even with the aid of scanners, was no picnic, but with the prospect of coming face to face with that monster eel into the bargain...

"We'll take a chance and use the searchlight, Phones," he said, "The quicker we get through the better, I'm thinking."

"That's one proposition I'm not voting against," Phones gave his cheerful grin. "Let's go!"

The tunnel rose slightly, which accounted for the silt not slipping down it. Soon there was bare rock all around them. The average diameter was about twelve feet– wide enough to allow passage to that monster eel, and it was unlikely there would be any tight bends for the 'sprite to negotiate.

Phones switched on the hydrophone speaker and Troy could hear for himself the muffled tolling of the bell. It was irregular as if being tugged by an underwater current of inconstant velocity. The sound was gradually loudening.

About three hundred yards along the tunnel the walls fanned out into another cavern. Troy saw a large opening just within the range of the searchlight before he switched it and the cabin light off so they would not offer a target for the monster eel if it should be lurking there.

They glided forward towards the cavern opening. The pinging of the scanners mingled with the deeper tone of the invisible bells.

As they emerged the 'ping-ping' of the scanners became less frequent.

"We're in something pretty big," Phones said. "Mostly solid rock, but I'm getting other soundings, too. Metal and wood, just like a wreck."

"It's not likely to be that, Phones," Troy said, excitement edging his voice. "Seems as though we've arrived. Stand by. I'm going to risk the searchlight."

As the light fired out, Troy swivelled it round. Pushing back the darkness, they peered out eagerly. Fish darted away from the glare. A large deep-sea squid stared down the beam with malignant saucer eyes and darted away with tentacles writhing.

"Looks as though we won't be short of company, anyway," Phones grunted.

"He's bigger than us, so we can get out the way he got in."

"Troy! Look!" Phones suddenly yelled. "Bring that beam around a point or two to starboard."

Troy obeyed and then saw what had excited his friend. Bathed in the light of the beam was the white tower of an old Spanish style church, canted at an angle like the leaning tower of Pisa. It was truncated as though the uppermost portion bearing the spire had fallen off.

In the two tall narrow arches of the belfry, massive bells swung ponderously. The sound was now loud in the speakers and Phones switched off the hydrophone before giving his Captain a disappointed look.

"Sure doesn't look much like a cathedral to me," he said.

"It probably never was anything more than a church," Troy said. "The legend promoted it to cathedral. Let's take a closer look."

They cruised up to the tower. It was made of solid hewn stone blocks encrusted now with coraline marine growths blazing in rainbow colours as the light touched on them. The bells themselves were in good condition, for their bronze castings had resisted the corrosive effects of sea and time. Fish darted in and out of the belfry just as birds must have flown long ago.

"Gee!" Phones said wonderingly. "Five hundred years back it was way up there on the coast. Then, as that guy Manco said, the earth shook itself and—wham!"

"Yeah. Guess ours must be the first human eyes to see it since."

Troy swung the light beam downwards. The fallen top of the tower lay in a heap of stone blocks. A paved road, half-buried in silt, and sloping at a crazy angle, led away from it, flanked by the tumbled ruins of stone buildings and huge baulks of rotting, worm-eaten timber which marked where adobe buildings had once stood.

They followed the course of the curving road through that ghost of an ancient town, where Cortez, the conqueror of Peru himself, might have trod.

They saw the half-buried skeletons of humans and horses, the remnants of a wagon, a corroded helmet and breastplate once worn by a conquistador.

Further down, where the old shoreline must have been, were the massive timbers of what had been a jetty, broken and jumbled like matchsticks. Crushed between it and a rock wall was the rotting encrusted hulk of a once-proud galleon of Spain.

A corroded cannon lay on its side on a stone quay, with cannonballs strewn beside it.

Further back beyond the quay were the partly demolished walls of a massive stone building that had probably been a warehouse. This, if anywhere, Troy thought, would be where the treasure would be found, stored awaiting shipment to Spain. Maybe this galleon was on a transport mission like that when it had been caught in the harbour during the earthquake.

He took the 'sprite lower, down between the broken walls. In the light, he could see bits of rotten wood among oblong heaps.

"Guess that wood could be the remains of bullion chests, Troy."

"Yeah. And those black lumps could be the bullion coated with silver sulphide. I've seen it like that in wrecks. The stuff should be all right inside."

"Well, there's sure a fortune to be picked up here, Troy. Hagen knew he wasn't on a wild goose chase."

"Sure. But he's not getting it if we can help it, Phones. Guess we'd better start looking for that way out."

They were climbing past the belfry when the forward scanner chimed urgently.

"Stand by!" Phones yelled. "Douse the light!"

Troy barely had time to switch off the searchlight before something crashed into the aquasprite, sending it tumbling over and over through the dark water.

Phones cannoned against Troy, knocking his hands from the controls. Helpless, they whirled around. Hanging upside down in his seat straps, Troy got a glimpse of a massive ribbon-finned back flashing past below in the cabin light.

His throat went tight. They'd been crazy to linger so long among the ruins with the searchlight blazing.

Phones sagged against his straps, blood trickling from his temple where he had struck it against the control bank. Troy reached the controls with an effort and righted the little craft. Phones slumped back. He was out cold.

Troy heard the scanners pinging again, and out of the corner of his eye, he saw the great eel rushing at them. He flicked off the cabin light and sent the 'sprite into a steep climb. The conger hurtled past, swerving aside just in time to avoid crashing into the belfry. The surging pressure wave caused by the charge set the bells clanging urgently.

The eel came round and up with incredible swiftness, Troy thought it must have caught a glimpse of the faint lights on the instrument panel.

He dived below it, and it blundered on into the darkness. Troy had little doubt he could evade the clumsy charges of the giant fish, barring accidents.

Barring accidents!

As Troy brought the 'sprite up out of the dive, his stomach contracted into a cold knot of fear. In the dim light, he saw a tiny jet of water spurting beyond Phones' unconscious figure.

The 'sprite had sprung a leak between the transparent casing and the hull—maybe due to the colossal blow from the eel's head. It was a miracle the little craft had not burst like a balloon.

If Phones had been conscious he might have been able to plug the leak temporarily, but Troy couldn't do it and handle the craft at the same time—not with that monster already charging down at him again.

He couldn't see it, but he could feel the pressure wave building up against the hull and hear the frantic alert from the instruments.

Troy knew that any sharp turn or sudden acceleration might burst that seam wide open. He and Phones wouldn't last a minute then.

He saw the belfry before him and made for it. There was just one chance. If he could shelter from the monster and plug that leak!

The conger snaked after him.

The 'sprite sped into one of the belfry arches with feet to spare. Troy fired the retro-hydrojets to check it. The great snout of the conger struck the tower, rocking it.

The eel drew off and charged again, seemingly oblivious to pain or shock. Troy heard what sounded like screeches of rage. The whole tower seemed to be quaking.

He saw the dark shape coming again. Another blow might send the tower, weakened by centuries of water pressure, tumbling to join the ruins below, crushing the little eggshell of a craft.

Troy turned the 'sprite to face the charging monster and triggered both missiles, straight at the gaping mouth that he could dimly see. If they had been Stingray's missiles, he would have had no doubt of the result, but these miniature torpedoes could have deterrent value only against such a brute.

He lost sight of the missiles as they flashed from the belfry, but an instant later he saw the double explosion light up the dark cavern of the creature's mouth.

For a moment there seemed to be no effect and then suddenly the conger lost momentum and veered away to vanish into the darkness. It didn't come back.

Troy cuffed the sweat from his brow.

Then, his blood seemed to turn to ice in his veins. Even above the muffled booming of the great bells outside the hull, he could hear the rush of flowing water.

He switched on the cabin light. Water was spurting through an inch wide split, a split that seemed to grow before his eyes with horrifying speed.

Phones groaned and the sound drove Troy into frantic action. He grabbed his friend's mask and thrust it over his face.

"Wake up, pal!" he yelled. "We've got to get out of here!"

Chapter Eleven
SUBMARINE SHOWDOWN

When Phones' face mask was secure, Troy pumped a shot of oxygen into it, and as he tightened his own mask he saw with relief that Phones was waking up. The water surging through the rent in the aquasprite was now up to their calves.

"Come on, Phones!" he said urgently, shaking his friend's shoulder. "Get your flippers on. We've got to abandon ship."

Phones didn't waste time asking questions. He could size up the situation for himself. They pulled on their flippers, and then Troy prepared the emergency release.

"Ready?" he asked, "Releasing hatch!"

Pulling on a heavy duty red lever, he released the seal around the canopy. The cabin flooded in seconds. As soon as the pressure was equalized, he opened the casing and they floated out of the waterlogged craft.

Amid the clangour of the bells above them, it was impossible to communicate on the hydrophones, and they swam clear of the belfry.

"Thanks, pal!" Phones gasped when he could make himself heard. "What happened to that conger?"

Troy told him. "I'm hoping he's finished, but we can't bank on that. We've got to find a way out of here fast. We'll have to take a chance with the torches, Phones."

They had seen enough in the beam of the searchlight to know they were in a vast submarine chamber. It wasn't a cavern, but more like a section of a wide steep-walled canyon which had been blocked off and roofed over by some freak of an earthquake long ago, entombing the ruins of the ancient town and perhaps preserving them.

But there had to be a way into it apart from the narrow channel by which they had arrived in the 'sprite, or the giant conger could never have got down to them.

They swam towards the roof, playing their torch beams about. It was a nerve-racking experience, having to be constantly on the alert against hideous death hurtling at them from the darkness. If the conger had survived that torpedo attack, they doubted whether their weapons would do more than tickle it or prod it into even greater fury.

Sooner than they expected, they found what they were seeking in one corner of the chamber where a wide fissure in the wall met the roof. It was wide enough to take Stingray, Troy thought, and there was a strong flow of current into it. This proved there was an outlet along the passage.

They swam through, keeping close to the bottom of the fissure, which ran almost horizontally, but twisted constantly in their torch beams.

Suddenly Phones shouted out, "Troy! Something's coming! I can feel the pressure wave."

Troy felt it at the same moment and his throat tightened. It had to be something pretty big to make a pressure wave felt against the flow of the current. What if it was the conger?

He flashed his torch about him, looking for a hole in which they could shelter. But there was none.

Then a voice came over the hydrophone.

"Stingray calling Troy! Stingray calling——"

"Atlanta!" Troy and Phones yelled joyfully in unison.

Presently they saw the probing beams of the super sub's searchlight, and then the gleaming bow of the craft nosed around a bend just ahead. A few moments later they emerged from the airlock and entered the control cabin.

"Good for you!" Troy told the smiling ladies. He briefly told them what had happened after they'd been trapped by the underwater avalanche. "You didn't meet up with that overgrown eel on your way through?"

"Does it look like it?" Atlanta grinned. "I'd still be quivering like a jelly."

"Then either he's finished or he's got some other hidey-hole where he's nursing a whale of a toothache," Troy said, taking over the controls from Marina.

"What now?" Phones asked.

"We're going back." Troy glanced at the chronometer. "Right now it's dawn topside. That means Hagen and his bunch of piranhas will be heading this way soon. Ten to one they'll find this route through to Sanito. We'll wait for 'em. Guess we've got a better chance of springing a surprise on them down there than out in the deep where their scanners can pick us up."

"What if that conger's still on the prowl?" Phones asked.

"A sting missile ought to take care of him. Let's go! I've got another hunch, Phones."

"Another? Why don't you quit while you're ahead?"

"Because I've a feeling that this is going to be the big showdown."

Troy took Stingray down over Sanito so that Atlanta and Marina could see the submerged site for themselves. They stared in wonder at the underwater town and treasure ship. Next, the Stingray crew grounded the vessel on the silt at a point farthest removed from the ruins.

As the lights, except those on the instrument bank, were switched off and they settled down to wait, Phones said, "What's the drill, Troy?"

"As I said earlier, I want to take Hagen and his daughter back to Marineville, and Number Thirteen too, if I can."

"A tough chore, Troy. Hagen's not going to hand it to you on a plate."

"Nope. We'll have to see how the cards stack up and play them accordingly."

The seconds ticked away into minutes and the minutes dragged into half-an-hour. Once something nosed the submarine curiously, and then the suckered tentacle of a squid explored the window of the cabin, but the creature soon withdrew, as if Stingray was deemed unpalatable. The only other sign of life they saw were small luminous creatures floating past.

"What if Hagen doesn't find his way down here?" Atlanta asked at last.

"Guess we'll have to go out and look for him. He'll be around somewhere. He won't pull out till he's found Sanito's treasure."

Another ten minutes idled away, and then Phones said, "I'm picking up an engine beat, Troy."

"Reckon this must be it. Stand by– action stations!"

Phones switched on the hydrophone speaker. The rhythm grew louder. There was no doubt in any of their minds now– the sound was unmistakably that of the other WASP vessel.

Then Marina grabbed Troy's arm and in the dim light, he saw her pointing up towards the invisible roof of the chamber.

A faint glow of light had appeared in the darkness. Troy knew it wasn't the luminescence of an underwater creature.

Presently, the beam of a searchlight was plainly visible and then the scanners began picking up the other craft. Until this moment, Number Thirteen had been screened from the echo beam by the rock passage through which it had been approaching.

Slowly, the hi-jacked sub descended. They could make out its lighted cabin and the streamlined shape behind the probing searchlight beam.

It spiralled, and for a moment Troy was scared the beam might reveal Stingray, but it swept well overhead. He got a glimpse of Hagen at the controls, with Helga in the navigator's seat beside him and four dimmer figures behind.

Six to four! Tough odds when five of those six were ruthless thugs who would stop at nothing. And Troy wasn't sure Helga was much better.

Only if it came to a showdown between the two subs would the chances be weighed in favour of Troy and his companions.

Number Thirteen circled above the ruins of the stone warehouse where Troy and Phones had seen the blackened masses of silver bullion. At last, the craft settled on its skids a short distance away from the ruins, its searchlight playing on them.

"Those cards are stacking up fast," Phones muttered. "Any ideas yet how we're going to play 'em, Troy?"

"Nope! We'll let 'em make the first move."

The other submarine was too far away for Troy to see what was going on in its control cabin but presently four figures in swim gear swam out of an airlock, with lighted headlamps and other equipment.

"They're making for the ruined warehouse," Atlanta observed.

"Work party," Troy mused. "Hagen's not going to waste any time getting that loot aboard."

"Will he be able to load it all in one trip?" Phones asked.

"Reckon not, but I've got an idea. Take over Stingray, girls! Put on your swim gear again, Phones. We're going to take a little trip."

As they put on their scuba equipment, Troy outlined his plan.

"That's WASP gear from Number Thirteen's equipment bay those guys are wearing, exactly the same as ours, Phones. If we join them…"

"They won't know us from the next guy, huh?"

"That's it."

"But I guess they can count, Troy," Atlanta said.

"I'm not that dumb," Troy grinned. "There won't be any more than four guys together in there at one time. But one of those that goes back into Number Thirteen won't be the one who came out."

"It's an awful risk," Atlanta protested.

"There's no other way to get into that craft and get the drop on Hagen," Troy said soberly, checking his sidearm. "We'd better get our drill right before we leave, Phones. Out there we'll have to communicate by signs and touch, in case they pick up our voices on their hydrophones."

A few minutes later Troy and Phones swam off and made their way through the darkness well out of the range of the lights of Number Thirteen. They came through the wreckage of the jetty and approached the ruins of the warehouse from the opposite end to where Number Thirteen was stationed.

Warily, they raised themselves and peered through a gap in the broken wall. The four divers were busy in the light of their torches, levering up the black lumps which were cemented by marine growths to the floor of the warehouse.

The divers loaded two of the lumps into a sling attached to a balloon, which one of them then inflated with air from the regulator of his swim gear.

The man swam off towards the submarine, towing the balloon and its cargo effortlessly.

Troy and Phones floated in the darkness, watching while two of the men took it in turns to take loads of the blackened silver to the submarine, and the other two men, wearing weighted belts, levered the lumps from the warehouse floor.

Presently, Troy touched Phones on the arm and motioned to him to follow. They swam round the rear of the ruined warehouse. Troy had noticed that the direct route the men took to the hold airlock of the submarine lay for part of the way in complete darkness, out of sight of the cabin of the craft.

He and Phones crouched down behind a fallen block of masonry and waited. There was no need for him to say anything, because his friend knew, from the briefing before they left Stingray, just what was required of him.

After a few moments, the head lantern of a returning diver showed up. They crouched well down out of sight. Then, as the unsuspecting man swam past, they were on him. Before he could cry out, Phones had snipped the microphone lead of his hydrophone with a wire-cutter, and the next moment Troy had jabbed home the needle of a hypodermic containing a powerful knock-out drug. A few spasmodic jerks and the man was unconscious.

Troy extinguished the man's headlamp and at a signal from him, Phones swam off through the darkness towards Stingray, dragging the unconscious man behind him.

Switching on his own headlamp, Troy swam on towards the ruined warehouse, towing the balloon carrier.

As he drew near he could hear the men inside talking in Spanish.

"José's been a long time." He recognised the voice as that of Carlos, the knife thrower, and the one he regarded as the most dangerous of the villainous quartet.

"I don't trust him any more than I trust Hagen," said one of the others. "I wouldn't put it past them to leave us stranded here once they have got most of the stuff aboard."

"Perhaps it would be a good idea to keep José here, levering up the silver," Carlos said thoughtfully. "Hagen we will deal with later. We need him to navigate the submarine, but once we are on the surface——"

He broke off as Troy swam into view between blocks of fallen masonry.

"You take your time, José!" Carlos growled.

Troy grunted something unintelligible, not wanting to give himself away by replying in a voice that was not José's. What he had overheard perturbed him. It was a threat to his carefully thought-out plan. If he was kept here…

He gave an involuntary gasp as Carlos deliberately flashed his lamp beam right into his eyes, dazzling him.

Carlos uttered an angry oath. "It is not José!" he cried. "Look! He is a spy!"

Troy sensed Carlos lunging at him. He saw the gleam of an upraised knife. He kicked away and Carlos, hampered by his weighted belt, missed by a foot.

One of the other men flung off his belt and dived at Troy, who twisted away as a knife sliced through the water close to his shoulder.

Desperately he fumbled with the flap of his holster. His plan could never succeed now and there was only one way out for him.

But before he could get the gun out, the other two men were closing on him. He darted away, frantically looking for someplace where he could hole up and call to Phones for help. The third man, swimming fast, was cutting across to head him off.

Then there was a flurry in the dark water above them and a great shape swooped down, vast mouth agape. With a scream of terror, the man cutting in front of Troy disappeared into it.

Troy's blood ran cold when he saw that the monster eel was turning, coming straight at him. Intuitively, he switched off his headlamp and dived straight down. He felt the lower fin of the huge creature rasp like a file along his legs, and then another blood-curdling scream told him that it had claimed a second victim.

As Troy grazed the bottom and twisted up again, he sensed something cleaving through the water nearby. Against the light from the submarine, he saw that it was the third diver. Evidently, he had followed Troy's example, had switched off his headlamp and was now desperately making for the safety of Number Thirteen.

Troy hesitated only a moment, then swam after the other man. As long as that conger was not seeking further prey, fate might have played into his hands after all.

The man swam into the open airlock and Troy was close behind his flippered feet. The lock was in darkness and Troy could hear the man panting hoarsely as he operated the hatch.

Did the man know he was there?

The matter was put beyond doubt a moment later. As the air hissed into the small compartment, the light came on. Up to his chest in the fast-receding water, Carlos was facing him.

With a snarl of rage, Carlos streaked his hand towards his neck just above his air cylinders.

Troy didn't wait for that hand to reach the throwing knife. He dived down, straight between the other man's legs, knocking him off balance and back against the bulkhead. Before Carlos could recover Troy had jabbed his hypodermic into the fleshy thigh. A brief struggle and Carlos went limp.

When the airlock was empty, Troy left Carlos lying there unconscious and, taking off his flippers and mask, went through the inner hatch into the lower deck.

Above he could hear Hagen's angry voice. "Where the blazes have those skunks got to?"

Drawing his gun, Troy raced silently up the companionway to the control cabin.

Hagen was on his feet, peering through the forward window towards the ruins of the warehouse, his daughter beside him.

"What goes on out there?" he growled.

"Guess your sidekicks have had a little grief, Hagen," Troy said quietly.

With a snarl of rage, Hagen swung round, his hand clawing a gun from the holster at his hip.

A blast from Troy's gun struck Hagen's arm. He gave a screech of pain and his weapon dropped from nerveless fingers.

"Just a friendly warning shot, Hagen," Troy said flatly. "Lucky for you I'm a gentle kind of guy or I might have done some real damage."

He smiled at Helga, who was cowering back against the far window, her blue eyes blazing.

"This is where we came in, I guess, Miss Hagen. Get a rope from that locker and tie up your father—and no tricks."

Sullenly, she obeyed, but Troy stood over her to make sure she made a good job of it.

Thoroughly scared now, she put up no resistance when Troy bound her own hands behind her.

He had just finished when a crash rocked the vessel, almost heeling it over. Helga screamed with terror as she and Troy were flung across the cabin.

Troy looked up to see the giant conger hurtling away through the searchlight beam. He sprang into the pilot's seat. The maddened creature might seriously damage the craft and he wanted to make good his promise to Commander Shore to take it back to Marineville.

He triggered the motors and the submarine shot forward, lifting sharply off the silt, just as the conger charged again. The creature missed by feet, swung ponderously, and came in pursuit.

Troy flung the sub into a loop, cursing softly when it responded with irritating slowness compared with Stingray, but he got above the giant eel and then, as it turned for a third charge, he got it dead in the sights of the port missile.

"Sorry, pal!" he muttered. "You saved my life back there in a back-handed way, but you've sure asked for this."

The torpedo was heading straight into the gaping mouth and Troy expected the explosion to blow off the great head. But with a sudden convulsive jerk of powerful muscles, the huge sinuous beast turned sharply and vanished into the darkness below.

The missile struck a rock wall, opening a pathway to the open sea. As Troy gave a low whistle of surprise, impressed by the monster's speed and reflexes, he saw the giant conger disappear into the freshly blasted passageway.

He shook his head. "Guess we haven't seen the last of the Sanito monster!"

Troy picked up the hydrophone microphone.

"Wasp Thirteen to Stingray!" he said. "Phones and Marina report to take over the recaptured vessel."

As he swung the craft round to meet the approaching Stingray, he saw Hagen sneering up at him from the floor.

"You haven't won yet!" the other man snarled.

Troy chuckled. "Never thought a tough guy like you would believe in miracles, Hagen."

A few minutes later Troy handed over the controls of Number Thirteen to Phones and swam across to Stingray. He smiled at Atlanta as he slid into the pilot's seat beside her.

"There's nothing to touch Stingray, Atlanta. Those other craft seem like a million years behind the times after her," he said as he turned the nose of the super sub towards the fissure leading out of the great submarine chamber.

"What about the rest of the silver down there, Troy?"

"Guess it's been there five hundred years. It can wait till the proper department send out an expedition to pick it up. Right now we've got something far more precious to get back to your pa."

She smiled warmly. "You say the sweetest things, Troy!"

"Oh, I wasn't meaning you, honey!" he said solemnly. "I was thinking of Hagen."

She glared at him. "Why, you!"

The forward scanners pinged urgently, and she glanced at her instruments.

"Troy!" she gasped. "I'm getting metallic soundings, moving in fast."

"That means underwater craft."

And then Troy saw them in the extremity of the powerful searchlight beam, four of Titan's terror fish swooping down at him in open formation.

"Stand by for action, Phones!" he ordered.

"Okay, Troy!" came the reply over the hydrophone. "Two for you and two for me?"

"You pluck your chickens before you eat 'em!" growled Troy. "Spread out!"

Number Thirteen veered away from Stingray, seeking to divide the enemy. But to Troy's surprise all four terror fish kept on towards Stingray, and he saw that the centre pair were towing a big trawl net between them.

"Oh, no!" he muttered. "Not that again! Doesn't that shark Titan ever learn any new tricks?"

At that moment he recalled Hagen's sneering taunt. So this was what he'd meant.

"Titan must be in cahoots with Hagen," he told Atlanta. "They're not going after Thirteen because they think Hagen's in control of it. Stand by sting missiles, port and starboard."

"Standing by, Troy!"

A moment later the two centre vessels were right in the sights.

"Fire!" Troy commanded tersely, sending the slim deadly torpedoes swiftly to their targets.

The double explosion lit up the darkness of the great chamber and Stingray bucked in the pressure waves. The two escort vessels swung away from the glowing debris, one diving, the other climbing swiftly to get above Stingray.

"I'll take the high road, you take the low road!" Phones chanted.

"Okay!" Troy replied with a grin. "Hold tight, Atlanta!"

He sent the super sub screaming down after the terror fish. The aquaphibian pilot tried to climb again, but a sting missile struck its tail, blowing a gaping hole in the rear of the craft. The head, out of control, hurtled on into the rock wall and disintegrated in flame.

As the echoes faded over the hydrophone speaker, there was another muffled explosion from above, and flaming debris came drifting down.

"Number Thirteen to Stingray!" Phones reported cheerfully. "All enemy craft accounted for. Clear to go!"

* * *

A week later, in Marineville control tower, Commander Sam Shore threw down the pen with which he had just signed a lengthy report.

"That's the end of another chapter of WASP history," he pronounced with satisfaction. "Hagen got ten years, José and Carlos five apiece, and sweet little Helga two. That'll keep 'em out of trouble for a while, I guess."

He cocked a fond eye from under a bristling grey brow at Troy, who was standing before his desk with Marina and Phones.

"But I guess it would take more than a prison planet to keep you three out of trouble. Earth tremors, avalanches, monster sea anemones, giant congers, terror fish—by Neptune, next you'll be claiming danger money!"

THE END